P9-DXF-752

OTHER NOVELS
BY LOUIS NOWRA

Into That Forest

FOR ADULTS

The Misery of Beauty
Palu
Red Nights
Abaza
Ice

Prince of AFGHANISTAN

LOUIS NOWRA

ALLEN&UNWIN
SYDNEY · MELBOURNE · AUCKLAND · LONDON

First published in 2015

Copyright © Amanita Pty Ltd 2015

Allen & Unwin
83 Alexander Street
Crows Nest NSW 2065
Australia
Phone: (61 2) 8425 0100
Email: info@allenandunwin.com
Web: www.allenandunwin.com

A Cataloguing-in-Publication entry is available
from the National Library of Australia
www.trove.nla.gov.au

ISBN 978 1 74331 482 1

Teachers' notes available from www.allenandunwin.com

Cover and text design by Ruth Grüner
Cover images from Sven Dirks (front, landscape), MarkMirror (back, sky)
and iStockphoto; internal images from Master Sgt Andy Dunaway, US Air
Force (page i) and from iStockphoto plus ninjaMonkeyStudio (vi), MivPiv
(14, 156, 164), Elijahjohn (32), mbaysan (38), christophe.cerisier (46),
michaelbwatkins (56), AHDesignConcepts (62, 74), Maximilian_Clarke (102),
cassp (124), MarkMirror (142), DTStudios (170)
Set in 11 pt Sabon by Ruth Grüner
Printed in Australia by McPherson's Printing Group

5 7 9 10 8 6

TO BASIL, A MINIATURE PRINCE

1

I am falling from the sky. The cold air stings my face. After counting ten seconds I pull the rip cord, there's a sudden lurch upwards as the parachute opens, and I drop more slowly. The aeroplane noise fades away and the only sound is the 'chute snapping in the wind. A surge of adrenalin runs through me, but I force myself to breathe more calmly. I see black parachutes against a greenish moon. I recognise Casey because he's got his dog strapped to his chest. In the distance is the dark outline of the forest we will have to make our way through before reaching the target.

The ground looms up and I brace myself for a landing. I hit the earth with a thump and a breeze catches my parachute, forcing me to run a few steps before I deliberately fall, dragging it down with me. After freeing myself from the straps, I bundle up the 'chute and start for the trees, where I bury it as quickly as possible in the soft ground under the pine needles.

The others have landed and are joining up. Our radios are turned off and there are no voices, just the sounds of heavy boots moving quickly across the hard earth and grunts of effort. Like the others, I'm carrying an assault rifle and wearing body armour and night goggles. We must look like aliens in the green shimmering light as we gather on the treeline.

I join Casey and his dog, Prince, and give him a grin and a thumbs-up. I feel a tap on my shoulder. It's the leader of the rescue mission, Major Perry, an American. In his forties, he's as fit as a soldier half his age. He signals to me and Casey to make our way to the front of the team. There are probably no mines buried in the pine plantation, but Prince is leading the patrol just in case. His hearing is sharp enough to catch the very high-pitched whine produced when air moves over the thin wires of a booby trap. My job is to cover Casey and his dog in the raid.

Prince is not straining but the line is taut as he sniffs his way forward ten metres in front of Casey. It would be nearly impossible for me to see him without the night goggles. He is a black-and-tan Doberman pinscher and the white patch on his throat has been dyed black, as have the pockets of tan, to make him even less visible. He moves, as he always does, with a delicate gait, almost like a prance, as if his paws are barely touching the ground. In the eerie green glow his sharp pointed ears make him look like the devil. He weaves through the trees, sniffing the earth and air.

Although this is my first such mission, I'm not so much afraid as excited. The operation has happened quickly. A few weeks ago the Taliban kidnapped three doctors, two men and one woman, and they demanded $10 million ransom. In the video they sent, the hostages looked scared and exhausted. The latest phone intercepts have told us that the kidnappers are becoming tired of waiting for the money and are threatening to behead the doctors, one by one. The phone intercepts and drones have revealed the location. The team has been parachuted in, four kilometres from the target. We are to make our way through the pines, up a steep hill, raid the compound and liberate the doctors, and then head along a rocky escarpment to a small patch of level ground where the choppers can land to pick us up. The whole operation has to be done as quickly as possible because the one-kilometre hike to the pick-up site will be across open country where it will be easy to pick us off.

I've only had twenty-four hours to prepare for the mission. Originally the team was to have had an American handler but his dog died of a snake bite and Casey and I were brought in at the last moment. I may

3

be four years younger than Casey but I'm a good shot, much better than he is. When we hunted rabbits and wallabies together back home, he used to say I could shoot the balls off a mosquito at a hundred metres.

Halfway through the forest, Prince pauses. Casey holds up his hand for the others to stop. The dog is peering and sniffing at something but he hasn't frozen the way he does when he senses a buried mine. He sniffs the earth a few more times, then glances back at Casey and pulls on his lead, moving forward again. When I reach the spot where he stopped, I see the glowing green bones of a donkey's skeleton.

Glancing over my shoulder I see the other ten men are moving through the trees like black ghosts. The pine needles crunch underfoot and a fresh and clean smell fills my nostrils. It's so different from the usual stinks in the villages and towns.

As we near the clearing, my heart begins to pound. The whole raid depends upon surprise and perfect timing, not only to carry out the rescue itself but to reach the rendezvous point before dawn. From here we have to walk up a bare hill, hoping not to be seen. If anyone up there in the compound cared to look we'd be easy to spot, and that'd be the end of us all.

Major Perry joins me and whispers, in that slow

southern drawl of his, for me and Casey to take up our positions. We join the ragged line of soldiers, silently marching up the slope.

The night goggles bathe everything in lime green. It's as if I'm walking on the bottom of the sea. It's hard to keep my footing on the shifting shale. The air is cold, but even so I can feel the beads of sweat dripping from my underarms. There's so much at stake and everything has to go right.

I look up and I'm surprised at how shiny the waxing moon is. It seems as bright as a searchlight. I instinctively crouch as I move up the slope. I can only hope the kidnappers are asleep up there.

The slope eases and I can see a mudbrick compound has been built into the side of a hill. As it comes into view we begin to move into our assigned positions. At least there are no lights visible, which means they still haven't seen us.

Two soldiers attach plastic explosives to the wooden gate. I take up my spot further along the mud wall, away from the blast. The Americans will go in first. Casey and I are to search for the hostages in the rear buildings. Casey pulls out a piece of checked shirt which belonged to one of the doctors and gives it to Prince to sniff. At the same time Casey strokes Prince's withers to let him know something is about to happen and to be calm. Major Perry raises his hand. I feel myself tense and realise I'm licking my dry lips.

Major Perry drops his hand and a moment later the earth rocks. At the same time there's a piercing white light, the sounds of crashing metal and wood and the yell of *It's on!* Closely following Casey and Prince, I rush into the compound, jumping over the smouldering ruins of the gate.

The noise and light is unbelievable; grenade blasts, gunfire, screams and shouts, like the noisiest light show and rock concert ever. There's no time to be afraid. I know what to do as Casey orders Prince to sit. I rip off a piece of plastic sheeting from one of the compound windows and Casey runs to it with Prince in his arms, then hurls him through the narrow gap. *Atta boy! Go!* he yells. We have practised this many times and Prince knows what to do, but this will be his first time in a real battle – as it is mine.

From inside come cries of fear and ferocious barking as he terrorises the occupants, exactly as he has been taught. I run around to the side with Casey, rip a blanket away from a doorway and rush in. I can hear Prince barking in the next room and when I enter it I see two bare-chested Taliban pinned against the wall, screeching and shouting at him, holding their hands in front of their groins to protect themselves. *On the floor! On the floor!* I yell in Pashto above the noise. They obey me immediately. Time is of the essence so I leave Casey and Prince to look after the situation while I clear the next room – but then the dog races past me. *Prince! Back! Prince!* I hear Casey crying out. I jump to the side of the doorframe, take a deep breath and leap into the room to see a white woman cringing and screaming in fear, while Prince snarls and springs at an armed man wearing a black turban, who has his rifle raised to shoot. I have a split second to aim. There's a loud crack and the slight bump of my rifle against my shoulder. The man slaps his head as if he has forgotten something and slumps to the floor. I'm stunned and stand rooted to the spot, paralysed by what I have done. I have never shot a man before.

The sound of crying jolts me out of my shock and I see two white men and a white woman pressed up against the far wall: the three hostages. *It's all right, it's all right, we're getting you out of here!* I shout over the noise and point them in the direction I've come. *Out that way!* In the chaos I spot Prince sniffing the dead body and hear Casey calling him, *Come on, boy, let's go!* Prince runs back into the other room as I follow the hostages outside, stumbling past Casey, who's finishing handcuffing the two insurgents with hard plastic bands, wrestling their arms behind their backs, forcing them to lie on their stomachs.

I join the hostages outside, with Casey and Prince bringing up the rear. It's bedlam. Explosions, heaving earth, and tracer lights zipping everywhere. Two Afghan women in burqas are huddled with their children against a wall, screaming and crying. They shouldn't be here. We had been told there were no families in the compound. Bullets rip up the ground around me. *Frag out!* someone yells and I instinctively drop to the ground, as do Casey and Prince. Rooms explode one after another. There is a brief pause and then cries of *Clear! Clear!*

Black smoke is pouring out of the windows and doorways and billowing into the sky. Another huge blast rocks the compound and talc-like dust rains down on me. A Taliban soldier bursts out of a burning room, a rocket strapped to his back. He reaches for the trigger on his grenade launcher. An American soldier, a few metres away from me, falls to one knee and fires a rocket-propelled grenade at the insurgent, who explodes in a bright flash. Bolts of fire shoot out of his backpack, as if he's a giant sparkler.

A calm Major Perry jogs over to me as if he's merely on a training exercise, and, not even raising his voice, says to the hostages who are crouching in a squatting position behind me and Casey, *We're getting you out of here*. Then he shouts an order to four of his men to come across the yard to us. *Ma'am, sirs,* drawls the Major, *go with them*. The three doctors, dazed by their sudden rescue and the firefight, obediently hurry after the American soldiers. *You two Aussies*, he orders us, *oversee the dust-off and leave on the second chopper*.

Casey and I join the hostages, who are panting with terror and effort, trying to keep up with their rescuers. *Where are we going?* asks one of the doctors, his eyes scanning the night sky for helicopters. I point to the ridge, then glance at my watch. It's not too bad, we're only a few minutes behind schedule, but soon we're going to run out of darkness. The sun will rise in about twenty minutes and that means we have to make the target area in fifteen.

With the weight of our body armour and knapsacks, the physical effort is so taxing that no one talks. My lungs seem near bursting and it's all I can do not to slip on the rocks and shale. Prince runs alongside Casey with that steady, effortless canter of his. I can hear more blasts behind us as the Americans methodically blow up the rest of the compound.

On reaching the ridge we run onto a small patch of flat earth as a helicopter comes closer, the sound of its high-pitched rotor blades echoing around the hills. The Americans push the doctors to the edge of the landing ground, which is just large enough to take one chopper at a time, and order them to turn their backs. The chopper descends, sending dirt and grit everywhere and blasting the backs of the flinching doctors, who, unlike us, have no body armour.

As soon as the chopper lands the soldiers push the hostages towards it and bundle them in. Everything has to be done as fast as possible, in case of mortar or rocket attack. The four Americans scramble in after the doctors and the helicopter dusts-off in a blizzard of dust and pebbles. I watch it rise into the pale sky. *Good dog, good dog*, I hear Casey murmuring to Prince as he strokes his neck. In the distance I see the Americans hurrying up to the ridge from the burning compound just in time for the second helicopter, which is hovering above us. The mission is going perfectly.

I jump as bullets kick dust up around my feet. Two Taliban are coming up the ridge, chasing after the second team and shooting at them. There's another blast of grit and pebbles as the chopper lands. The Americans come into view, racing to the landing spot. I peer into the green darkness – where is Casey? I see a running figure and recognise that it's him hurrying back to cover the Americans as they come upon the ridge. Prince is loping after him when Casey seems to trip and fall. He's been hit.

I set off, sprinting like a madman to him, my heart pounding as if it's going to burst out of my rib cage. The two Taliban are coming up onto the ridge. I stop and shoot at one. The bullet hits him in the chest and he falls to the earth. I turn to see the second already kneeling and aiming his grenade launcher. Out of the corner of my eye I see Casey suddenly sit up and point his rifle; there is the crack of his gun and the Taliban falls sideways, firing as he does so. I flinch. The grenade flies over my head and hits the chopper. There is a blinding light and a roar like the earth splitting open. Hundreds of needles slam into my body. The heat from the explosion burns my mouth. The air is sucked out of my lungs.

When I wake up, I see a shattered green-and-black world. I shake my head, trying to make sense of what I'm seeing. It's like looking through a spiderweb or a kaleidoscope of jumbled pieces. Then it dawns on me; my night goggles have been shattered by shrapnel. I tear them off and I find myself blinking at the intense white-and-orange light of the helicopter burning fiercely, its shell a furnace of melting metal, with acrid smoke and the stink of petrol in the air. The grenade must have made a direct hit on the petrol tank. No way could any of the Americans have survived. It's as if they have been vaporised.

What jolts me next is the sudden realisation that I can't hear a sound. The explosion must have deafened me. Everything is silent. But I have to keep going. I stumble along the ridge to Casey, dreading what I will find.

There are no signs of wounds or blood on his body. I rip off his night goggles. His eyes are open, and bright with the reflection of the burning wreck – but his throat has a bleeding hole the size of a ten-cent coin. He seems to recognise me and smiles, then his eyes begin to close. *Don't close your eyes! Don't close your eyes!* I'm screaming as I shake him. But there's no reaction. Since I've been here I've heard every soldier say that no man should die alone. I kneel beside him and hold his hand. *Come on, live. Casey, you gotta live!* I plead. But his eyes close and his body goes limp. I take several deep breaths to calm myself. It's then I spot three more Taliban coming up the ridge. I have to leave Casey and save myself.

I run back to the landing spot only to see Prince on the opposite side of the fiery wreck, trotting off into the flickering shadows. I call out to him but he pays no attention. When I catch up with him and seize him by the collar he spins around, baring his teeth and is about to launch himself at me when he realises who it is. He steps away, panting and yawning; I know this is his way of trying to calm himself. He shakes his head and sits staring at the ground, seemingly unaware of the dangers around him. I lift him up by the collar but he sinks down again as if incredibly tired. The Taliban soldiers are coming closer. I'm desperate. I shout at Prince and shake him but he continues to stare at the ground. *Prince! Come!* I yell in his ear, but still he doesn't react. He must be in shock. Then I see why: there's a giant clump of blood matting his right flank. He's been shot.

I'm shaking with panic. I have to save myself but I can't leave him to lie here or be killed. But how to get him moving? I jump in front of him and lift his head so he's facing me. His eyes are blank. This is terrible. I don't know what to do. Then I remember something Casey told me. I spit into Prince's face, but he doesn't react. *Get up! Get up!* I yell at him. I'm frantic with fear and spit into his face again. Prince shakes his head and jumps up, baring his teeth at me. Tiny spurts of earth jump up around me. There's no time to do anything but run. I grab him by the collar and push him in front of me. *Come on*, I feel myself shouting, and we head off up the hill into the darkness.

2

I feel even more scared because I can't hear. I have no idea if we are making a noise or if we are being followed. Prince stops. I grab him by the collar and force him to come with me. We keep to the dark side of the slope in an attempt to avoid the rising sun which is bathing the other side. It would be easier to walk along the top of the ridge, but our silhouettes would stand out against the morning light.

Finally I stop, too weary to go on. The adrenalin rush has faded, leaving me feeling exhausted and hollow. I signal Prince to sit. I can't see anyone following us but it's dark on this western side and the Taliban wear black, so they could be anywhere. Images of the chopper exploding and of Casey's death whirl through my mind. The realisation that I've killed two men unnerves me, even though they would have gladly killed me. My hands are trembling. I suck in a few deep breaths. I have to concentrate and figure a way out of this mess.

There's no doubt that the Americans will send recon-naissance planes and drones in to check if anyone has survived the inferno but all they'll see is the charred wreck of the second helicopter. They'll think no one has survived – and that means there's no hope of a rescue. I'm on my own – well, not quite; I've got Prince.

Somehow I have to make my way back through enemy territory. How can I do that without being seen? And how can I reach the closest allied base? The quick-est route back is probably across the ridge and over the mountain range beyond.

I begin to feel stinging sensations in my torso, and my left shoulder is sore. Prince licks gently at his wound. I need a refuge, somewhere for us both to recover before starting the journey home.

I'm weighing up my options when I'm jolted by the sight of silhouettes outlined against the harsh morning light – three Taliban carrying rifles and marching along the top of the ridge. I push Prince down onto his stomach and drop to the ground with him. Even if we stay where we are, on the dark side of the slope, the sun will soon make us easy to spot. I look back and see that the fires have faded and the compound is hidden in a thick black smoke.

It's a relief when the figures on the ridge grow smaller and vanish down the other side of the hill. They won't expect what we'll do next. We'll double back and retrace our steps. We have just enough time to reach the pine forest before the sun rises too high. I give Prince a reassuring pat on his head and tell him what a good boy he is. There's something puzzled about his look. I yell into his ear. He doesn't react. I think he's deaf like me. I stand up and motion him to follow. I do it again. He still doesn't move. I'm suddenly angry. I'm trying to save my own life and already he's becoming a burden. I grab his collar hard and pull but he sits staring at the ground. I pull again and he looks up, fearful; as if he's paralysed with shock. I curse him and yank him up with all the strength I've got. Pulling tightly on the collar, I make him walk until he realises he has to obey me. I let go of him and he trots obediently beside me.

We give a wide berth to the smouldering remains of the helicopter. A hundred metres further on is Casey's body. I stop, shocked by the sight of how lifeless and exposed to the elements it is. There's a sudden movement beside me and Prince runs to Casey. He sniffs at the body and scrapes his paw on Casey's leg as if trying to wake him. When that doesn't work, he frantically licks his face as if trying to give him life. The sight devastates me. I join Prince, who looks at me as if he thinks I can wake his master up. I feel like crying but there's nothing I can do for Casey. *So long, mate*, I hear myself say. Then I grab the reluctant Prince by the collar and drag him down the ridge.

We pause before the slope that leads to the pines. It's a kilometre hike down the hillside we came up. I'm hoping the billowing smoke in the compound will make seeing us difficult. It's a risk, but there's no alternative.

I tap Prince on the neck. He looks up at me and frowns, as if he too knows the dangers. He may be deaf but he seems focused on what we're doing. I bend over like a hunchback, hoping to be as inconspicuous as possible, and march down the slope. It's slow going and my left shoulder throbs with pain. Sometimes I look back to see if we're being followed but all I see are the compound walls and a dark fog of smoke, its bitter stink pinching my nose.

I'm grateful for one thing – that we are moving downhill. Still, it's difficult to negotiate it because the shale and stones are loose on the ground and it's impossible to rush without slipping and falling. The sun begins to shine on the top of the slope, the band of light trailing us. My shadow is hurrying ahead of me on the dead earth. *Faster, faster*, I tell myself. Prince is following his own shadow, which is several steps in front of him.

The block of trees comes into view – in there, somewhere, I hope is a hiding place. As we near the treeline I notice that Prince is limping; he's trying not to put weight on his front right leg. There is no time to stop and examine it; we have to get to the plantation. I silently urge Prince on. Despite being in pain he keeps up with me, as if he too knows that once we find a haven we can rest.

We reach the edge of the pine trees. I look back to make sure I haven't been seen. The sun is overhead now, already baking the soil. In the distance black smoke is still pouring into the bright blue sky.

In the shade of the forest it's cooler. I make for the far western side, where the map I studied for the raid showed a creek. The treetops block out most of the glare, so we walk through shadows and light until we come to the creek on the edge of the trees. It's barely two metres wide but is flowing swiftly with meltwater from the snow-capped mountains.

I sink to the ground. Prince limps to the edge of the creek and eagerly laps up the water. The fur on his right flank is matted with blood and insects are feasting on the wound. The sight makes me catch my breath. I crawl over to him and wave away the insects. *Poor, poor boy*, I say, forgetting he is deaf. I set about cleaning him up as quickly as possible so the wound doesn't fester.

As I'm squeezing and soaking my handkerchief in the chilly water I catch a reflection of myself and am shocked to see that my forehead is smeared with blood.

For a moment I think I've been shot, but looking closer, I notice that a small piece of my right ear has been torn or shot off and parts of it have blown onto my face. I glance down at my armour and see that it's been shredded by shrapnel; but an examination of my body will have to wait until I fix up Casey's dog.

I pause before starting, realising that I may have stroked and patted Prince but he doesn't know me well. Like all handlers, Casey didn't like his dog socialising too much with the other soldiers because it might weaken the bond between the two of them. As gently as possible I wash the drying blood from Prince's smooth black fur. He shivers when the freezing cold cloth touches his skin and shudders in pain when I brush across something hard. I wipe away the remaining blood and notice a slice of metal stuck in his flank. I motion him to stand still and closely examine the object poking out of the flesh. The only thing to do is to pull it out in one clean yank. It will cause less pain if I do it quickly. I hold the exposed piece of metal between my thumb and index finger, silently count to three and pull. Prince leaps into the air in agony, but I've managed to remove a piece of shrapnel the size of a dollar coin. I stroke him and soothe him, realising he has probably yelped. *Good boy, good boy*, I say, glancing around to make sure there is no one who heard the yowl. I toss the metal piece into the water and clean the wound. I'm frustrated because it continues to bleed, then I remember the small plastic bottle of Quick Clot powder in my kit. I rub it onto the wound as softly as I can, but even so Prince's eyes blink in pain.

When I finish, I feel Prince licking my hand, as if apologising for his outburst. I check his front leg. There's no wound but when I stroke it just above the knee his tongue darts in and out as if he is trying to override the agony. It seems he has strained a muscle, which will probably slow him down, but I can't worry about it now. I have to attend to myself.

With great effort, because of the pain in my shoulder, I remove my body armour. It looks as if it's been put through a mincer. Shrapnel pieces have savaged it. Without the armour I would be dead. I examine my radio and GPS system. Both have been ripped apart and are useless. I take off my shirt and I'm horrified by the sight of my torso, which is a latticework of cuts and yellow and black bruises. Worse are the three bumps in my rib cage. Pieces of metal must have ripped through the armour and pierced my skin. I feel them. They're too deeply embedded for me to do anything about them – only a surgeon can remove them.

The worst pain is in my left shoulder. Only by twisting my head as far as possible can I see the tip of a piece of metal sticking out of it, the wound leaking blood.

I have to remove it before it works its way further in and causes the wound to fester. My knife is razor-sharp but I can only sterilise it by washing it in the water. I find a stick the width of a cricket stump, put it in my mouth and bite down hard on it. Then I dig the knife blade into the flesh next to the metal fragment. The pain is almost unbearable. Blood pours from the wound. I feel myself wanting to pass out. *Get it out! Do it now!* I tell myself. I push the blade in further and prod at the shrapnel underneath it, until it begins to emerge from my flesh. I grab tightly and pull. The process is so agonising that my teeth snap the stick in two. But I've done it. I stare at the piece of metal, wet with blood and bits of flesh. I've been lucky; if the bullet had been a few centimetres to the right, it would probably have killed me. Prince picks up one piece of the stick and offers it to me as if he thinks I want it. In a daze of pain, all I can do is shake my head and he drops it. I wash the wound clean, dry it and sprinkle it with the Quick Clot. I have some bandages in my med kit and plaster one over the gash.

I swallow a morphine tablet to ease the pain and try to focus on my next step. Prince stares at me. His black eyes seem impenetrable, it's impossible to tell what he feels. Is he worried? Afraid? Grieving for Casey? Does he know I'm a friend and will he obey me? I feel flies feeding off the blood on my forehead. I kneel down

22

on the creek bank and dip my head under the water, then drop my head in the water again only to hear my ears 'pop', the way they do adjusting to air pressure in a plane. I lift my head out and, for a moment, I hear a strange noise, which makes no sense, then I realise it's the sound of the bubbling water heading downhill. I laugh and look across at Prince, who is frowning as if he's puzzled by my behaviour. *Hey, boy, I can hear!* I say, amazed at how loud I sound.

Relieved, I drink from my water canteen and examine my rations. There is precious little, as I took enough only for an in-and-out mission. There are some strips of beef jerky, a muesli bar and pieces of dry chicken. I go to eat the muesli bar when I see Prince staring intently at me. He must be hungry too. I give him three strips of beef jerky. He gulps them down while I chew on the muesli bar and study the small map I've brought with me. It seems we're some 110 kilometres from base. By following the valley system I can make it back in three or four days – that's if Prince and I stay healthy – but it will be dangerous because all along the way there are villages that are loyal to the Taliban, and even if they're not, the locals will be too afraid to offer me shelter. To avoid the villages I'll have to move higher up and follow the contours of the hills and mountains. It means the trip could take an extra two or three days.

It'll be safer to travel at night – there's less likelihood of being seen and I can avoid the boiling heat of the days. I check my guns. I've got 210 rounds in my M4, six magazines of thirty rounds each and a Glock pistol with two magazines. Strapped to my left leg is the first-aid kit containing field dressings, blood-clotting powder and painkillers.

Suddenly there's a crack, like a bullet. I duck, drag Prince down with me and peer through the trees to where the noise came from. A few hundred metres away a bearded man in a loose-fitting brown jacket, billowing white trousers and green turban is chopping a fallen log watched by a young boy, probably his son.

Over the next hour I see the boy carry the chopped wood to a small cart attached to a patient donkey. Sometimes he drops the wood as if it's too heavy or he's just clumsy. It's only after a time that I notice that the boy's left arm is a stump at the wrist.

The father and son work silently until, after filling the cart, they stroll out of the forest. The son begins to sing in a soft voice as they head down into the valley, the song fading away. I sigh with relief. Prince and I are alone again but I'll have to stay alert until night comes, when I'll set out. If I get too comfortable I will fall asleep, so I sit up against a fallen log and put two large sharp stones under my backside.

The events of the past few hours have been so wild and bloody that I haven't had time to think about them, but now the full horror of Casey's death hits me. It's impossible to believe he's gone. There was that amazing energy he had. When everyone else was beat and just wanted to rest in the shade, he'd be urging us on to the next rise. When he ate, it was with the quickness of a starving animal, and when we were hoping just to get through the day without stepping on landmines or being shot at he'd be yakking on about how, after serving in Afghanistan, he was going to start a macadamia farm (*Yeah*, we'd joke, *a nut farm for a nutcase*). But more than his irrepressible life force was a sense of duty and purpose that seemed much stronger than mine.

Before my tour, we had last seen each other when I was fifteen and he was nineteen. I had only been in Afghanistan for three days when I accidentally saw his name on a rollcall sheet. I had heard that he'd signed up a few years before but I didn't know he was a dog handler and had been in the country for several months.

After finding out he was in the same camp, I snuck into his sleeping quarters while he was having a shower and nailed his boots to the floor. I waited in the shadows of the room and watched him dress and then try to put on his boots. He pulled and pulled but couldn't lift them. He looked so puzzled that I burst out

25

laughing. He looked up at me as I stood, oh so casually leaning against the door frame. For a moment he didn't recognise me and then when he did he grinned and said, *I should have realised it was you, Mark. You did this to me twice back home and who would have done it to me a third time but you, smart-alec Hollis.*

Our four years of separation disappeared in a moment. We hugged and laughed. He was as fit and solid as I had known him. He even seemed taller. There was something about his maturity and weather-beaten face that made me seem like a kid. But then he had always seemed the responsible adult and me the slacker.

Over the next few months in Afghanistan we became as close as we had been back in Emerald Creek when we hunted together and his parents fed me. We lived in the Snowy Mountains, in a place nicknamed Burning Mountain. The town had boomed for fifty years but when the coalmine closed, many people left to find work, including Casey. I learned that he had ended up in Far North Queensland where his father worked in the tin mines. Casey didn't want to be a miner and signed up for army service. One day when we were on patrol I asked him why. *It's my duty to fight against terrorism*, he said, with an earnestness that was impossible to question.

I'd tease Casey about his closeness to Prince, asking when they were going to get married. They even showered and slept together. I called him the Black Prince, not only because of his colouring but his eyes. They're totally black and when he stares at you they seem to bore right through you. He doesn't seem to have pupils or irises. *He looks like, like really totally evil, does your Black Prince*, I'd josh Casey. *You thinking of eating me, boy?* I'd ask the dog. Sometimes I'd call him El Diablo after the Doberman in the movie *Beverly Hills Chihuahua*, and pretending to be a fearful Chihuahua I'd shiver when I was near him, saying in a mock Hispanic accent, *Don't kill me, El Diablo!* Casey would take it all in good part and stroke Prince, murmuring, *The Taliban are scared of El Diablo, aren't they?* And the dog would nuzzle his leg as if he understood the praise. Sometimes Casey would become serious and say, *He's not a dog, he's a soldier. Equal to if not better than you and me, Mark.*

It was not only his eyes that made Prince different but the fact that he is a Doberman pinscher. Most if not all the other war dogs are German Shepherds, Belgian Malinois or Retriever crosses. Before Casey began training to be a dog handler, he wanted a Labrador. He had one when he was living on Burning Mountain and I remember it as being smelly, warm-hearted and smart.

The first time I went out on patrol with Casey

I was astonished by Prince's ability. He found three explosive devices along just one road. His reward was an unusually shaped square ball that he loved to chase and catch. That night, as we were resting in an almond grove and Prince gnawed happily on the ball, Casey told me just how difficult the early days with Prince had been. When Casey began the handler program, Prince was the only dog offered to him, because the other handlers had rejected him.

In the beginning Prince showed no affection even when patted, and he wasn't enthusiastic about chasing balls, when once he had been. It seemed as if he'd never bond with Casey. His tail was a stump and it was impossible to know if he was wagging it, so a handler had no idea if he was enjoying his work. It was as if he had become bored by the whole thing, and if he was losing interest in the training process he'd be thrown off the course. Casey despaired, staying awake at night feeling a failure. *It was as if I didn't have what it took to be a dog handler,* he said.

One day he forgot to bring his regular ball and accidentally found an old tennis ball in a clump of grass near the training paddocks. It was tattered, with half of its surface eaten away by snails. He called out to Prince to chase it and threw the ball as long and as high as he could. Prince went after it without any enthusiasm.

When it hit the ground it bounced and Prince did a half-hearted leap at it, but because of the uneven surface the ball jumped off in the opposite direction, causing him to twist in mid-air. His jaws snapped shut but he failed to catch it. He threw himself at it on the next bounce, but again, the ball flew off in a direction he didn't expect. On the fourth bounce he caught it and instead of giving it back to Casey, ran around him in smaller and smaller circles until he stopped and dropped the ball at Casey's feet. *Boy, oh boy, was he excited*, Casey said, his eyes shining with happiness at the memory.

He threw the ball again and again but Prince didn't tire of the game; because that's what he liked – the very unpredictability of the bounce. After driving all over Sydney, Casey eventually found what he was after in a joke shop: a square vulcanised ball. The random bounce fascinated Prince and his work ethic returned.

At the end of a training exercise he'd rush up to Casey and sit, panting and drooling with excitement. Casey would tease him by tossing the ball from hand to hand and Prince's eyes would flick back and forth, as if watching a tennis game, until he was almost beside himself with excitement. Then Casey would throw it as far and high as possible and off Prince would go, careening across the paddock, chasing after the ball.

I had seen Prince jump after the bouncing square

ball, and suddenly rotate in mid-air as the ball shot off on a tangent he hadn't predicted. It was as if time stopped and Prince and the ball were stuck in an eternal moment, like a photograph. His body, twisting and turning in the air, his eager mouth wide open, was an expression of . . . well, the only word is *joy*.

By the time I arrived in Afghanistan the bond between man and dog was as strong as any human relationship I had ever seen. Casey and Prince were hardly out of each other's sight. It was as if they were an extension of each other and both knew that what they were doing in Afghanistan was a matter of life and death. *You must always trust the dog. Always,* Casey would tell me. *A dog is going to be right more times than you are.*

He noticed everything about Prince; any signs of fleas, skin problems, even his teeth. Everyone who met Prince commented on his eyes, the colour of black opal; they revealed nothing of what he was thinking and only reflected the curious human face staring at them. But Casey was convinced, despite my teasing, that some-times when the sun shone at a certain angle, he could look beneath the black film and see that the eyes were really a bright blue. *When I saw the blue I realised I was looking into his soul*, he said. Another time I would have made a crack about how silly the idea was of a dog having a soul, but I knew that I couldn't because it would be like me making fun of someone's religion.

And yet, despite being trained as an assault dog Prince was a gentle creature. Even when he attacked someone, he did it with what I can only call a sense of professionalism. He may have sounded savage but his emotions were under control and Casey could easily command him to stop. The only time Prince had, as Casey said, *lost it*, was when an Afghan spat in the dog's face. For some reason – maybe because it reminded him of something that had happened when he was a pup before he was sent to the pound – the spittle on his face drove him crazy and he leapt at the Afghan's throat, wanting to kill him, only for Casey to pull him back on the leash. *He's a Prince, and royalty don't like to be spat on,* he said proudly.

I look at Prince's eyes. They are as inscrutable and mysterious as ever. *Well, boyo,* I say as I pat him, *those black eyes are worthy of the name 'The Black Prince'.* I make soothing noises as I stroke him. He stares directly at me with a slight tilt of the head as if he is puzzled greatly about something. Just what does he make of his deafness? Is he even aware he can't hear?

3

When I wake up I flinch, startled to see those two black eyes, a handspan from my face, peering down at me. Prince is sniffing me loudly as if he is trying to figure out whether I'm dead or not. Despite the sharp rocks I fell asleep.

It's nearing dusk. Soon it will be time to set out. Prince limps over to the creek and gulps down more water. His sprain bothers me. Just how bad is it? We'll be walking for several days, maybe up to a week if we have to make detours. Is he capable of making it back with me? How much of a burden will he be on our way back to base?

Apart from the spitting episode, I've only seen him lose his cool once. We were on patrol near a marsh when we were ordered to investigate a track near a herd of cows. There were suspicions it could be mined. Prince was working, free of the leash, some twenty metres from Casey. He stopped when a cow strolled across in front of him. He was staring at it when there was a thud that shook the ground and a landmine blew the cow apart, scattering it in all directions, so that pieces of it flew past, just missing me. Casey ran forward, calling to Prince, who was half swimming, half running through the marsh, but the dog didn't hear. Casey ran into the water and struggled through the mud and rushes to him, until Prince finally stopped on hearing his name being called. I laughed when they came out of the marsh, muddy and wet, and both with what can only be described as embarrassed expressions, as if they had let each other down.

What will happen if Prince becomes spooked again? Even if he trusts me, he won't hear if I call him because he is deaf.

He finishes drinking water and comes up to me. I scratch his throat, which is still dyed black, and he closes his eyes in pleasure. *Now, boy*, I say, *it's all right. We're going to be all right.* I know he can't hear me but hope he understands me just by my touch.

The forest has darkened and through the spiky tree-tops I can see the first evening stars. It's time to go. I examine what is left of the rations in my field pack: a tiny block of barbecued beef, three pieces of dried chicken, a few slices of cheddar cheese, tea bags, matches and chewing gum. It will have to do until we find food over the next couple of days. I bury my body armour. It's useless as protection now and it'd be too heavy to wear on our trek back through enemy territory. I pick up my rifle. My heart starts to pound as it does whenever I run out onto the football ground for the start of a game. *Come on, Prince,* I say, tapping him on the back of the neck, *time to get cracking.*

I walk off towards the edge of the forest, only to sense that I am alone. I look back and see Prince attempting to follow me, but he is limping badly. I don't know what to do. He's going to slow me down something awful. It'll be hard enough for me to get back, let alone with such a liability. If I leave him here, the locals will either kill him or mistreat him – they don't like dogs. I sigh with exasperation. If he can't come with me, then I will have to shoot him. But I can't do that; Casey would stop at nothing to bring his dog back home with him, and I have to do the same.

His right leg is raised so it doesn't touch the ground. It must be very sore. There's only one thing I can do – and he must trust me even if it hurts. I get down on one knee. *Now, boy, this is going to hurt.* I gently run my hands up and down either side of his sprained leg. He shudders. But the good thing is that he doesn't move away. I rub the leg again, becoming more vigorous. Prince blinks in pain. I'm trying to warm the stiff muscles, as trainers do with me when I play football.

I continue the massage and Prince blinks less often.

I work on it for half an hour and then get him to walk in circles until he gradually becomes confident about putting weight on the leg. I pat him on the head. *Let's do it, Black Prince*, I say, and set off. He doesn't follow but sits in the same spot. I turn back. He seems confused. *Come on*, I say, patting my thigh as I saw Casey do when he wanted Prince to come to him. Finally he stands up and comes to me, nuzzling my hand with his moist nose. *Good boy, time to hit the road.*

4

We walk out of the forest and head down a grassy slope. We will follow the green zone – the farming land that follows the rivers and streams. The massage has worked, Prince seems to be able to put his weight on his leg and the prancing style of his stride has returned.

I can see the twinkling lights of a village. We are a long way from it, but I have to be extra careful and I stop occasionally to listen for unusual sounds. There are owls and the howling of distant wolves but no sounds of humans. The waxing moon is bright and I try to move through the shadows as much as I can.

The slope becomes a plain and my nose is filled with flowery scents so heady that I feel as though I'm entering a florist's. It's a poppy field. As I pass through the thigh-high crop there is the light tapping sound of poppy bulbs hitting one another, like someone lightly clicking their fingers. The field continues down to the stream, where I pause to peer across to the other side. There are the silhouettes of hundreds of trees. I listen closely.

The leaves ruffled by the slight cold breeze sound like a gentle rain.

I have no idea how deep the stream is but the water's freezing and I don't fancy getting wet. We walk along the bank until the stream narrows. There are three rocks perfectly placed in the water which are probably used as stepping stones for farmers to cross back and forth.

Prince follows me across to the other side and we enter an orchard. It's so dark that I have no idea what is growing. I reach up and pluck a fruit; it's a peach, slightly soft to touch. I hold it to my nose; it smells heavenly. I bite into it and the sweet, soft fruit and juice runs down my chin. It's as if I have never tasted a peach before; it's so delicious. I gobble down two more and give one to Prince, who takes one sniff at it and strides away. I collect some more peaches and stuff them in my pack.

We march through to the far side of the orchard and then up a slope and along a ridge, and then we stop. In front of us is a steep hill. I'm hoping we can find a place to hide on the other side.

The climb is slow work. It takes intense concentration to stop from slipping on the loose rocks and stones. The landscape is as bleak as the moon. By the time we reach the top I'm breathing heavily in the thin air and so is Prince; he's panting loudly, his tongue hanging out. Even though I'm weary and my shoulder is throbbing with pain, I'm pleased. We've achieved our goal on time and can rest for an hour or so before we go any further.

The remaining beef and chicken rations I give to Prince. They are barely enough for two mouthfuls. It's obvious that I'll have to find some proper food for him on the long march back to base. I eat another peach and relax. Above me the sky is filled with a blizzard of stars. Since arriving in Afghanistan I have been in awe of the night skies. The stars and moon seem to be within touching distance; so sharp, so bright. As I'm gazing at the brilliance I see the silhouette of a drone passing high overhead. There is no sense in becoming excited. All the evidence from allied planes and drones will point to the conclusion that we've died in the chopper explosion. There's no getting around it, Prince and I are on our own.

He dozes at my side, while I gaze in wonder at the heavens. The more I stare at the sky the more movements I see: falling stars, and the darting red and white dots of satellites. It makes me feel less alone. I look down into the valley and the only sign of human beings is a few dim points of light in a distant village. The bare, silent hills are empty of any life, but there's also a solitary beauty to the landscape that makes me feel as if we are above the violence and killing below.

Prince sits up. His nose twitches. I grab my rifle and listen. There is the faint clatter of footsteps on the shale. My heart quickens. I point my M4 in the direction of the sound, my finger against the trigger. Prince jumps up and peers into the shadows between the pools of moonlight. There is nothing for a moment and then the definite sound of feet on loose rock. I see a figure emerging from the shadows. I steady my rifle and aim. I am about to shoot when I notice that it isn't a human but some sort of animal. It comes closer, trotting surely across the ground. I begin to think I am hallucinating. It looks like the devil. Then as it steps into the moonlight I take my finger off the trigger. It's a wild goat with two curved horns. It stops in mid-step, astonished to see a human and a dog in its way. In one movement it jumps up, spins around in mid-air and hurtles off down the far slope, its panicked flight accompanied by the rattle of stones.

I laugh with relief. *Good Prince*, I purr, stroking him. I snap my fingers behind his ears but he doesn't react. He hadn't heard the goat, but smelt him. That's the great advantage dogs have over humans. If their hearing goes, their sense of smell more than overcomes what for us would be an awful disability.

It's time to be on the move again. I inspect Prince's

wound. It's still raw but closing up. I rub and warm his sprained leg while he waits patiently, as if he knows what I'm trying to do. Once I'm certain he's able to walk on it we set off through the cold night, hugging the contours of the hills above the narrow valley.

When the sun comes up, we still haven't found a hiding place. We have to hurry; in an hour or two the poppy fields will be swarming with workers and they will easily spot us against the barren landscape. There has to be a refuge somewhere. We struggle up the next hill. By the time we reach the top we're exhausted. The sun has yet to pierce the darkness of the other side. As I scan the horizon for a hiding place, I see, amidst the deep black shadows, what looks like a cave set in a bluff.

Prince must feel my sense of urgency, because he hurries along beside me, occasionally glancing up as if confirming with me that the situation is serious. When we near our goal the sunlight hits it and I realise it isn't a cave but the remains of a building overlooking the valley, maybe a fort. Coming closer I see that its stone walls are now hillocks of rubble and the large main building is in ruins. Only a part of the roof remains at the back. The litter of artillery shell casings and bullets on the ground are signs that there must have been a fierce battle for it. Everything is rusting or crumbling as if the battle happened years or even decades ago. I gaze down the hill at the distant specks working in the poppy fields. From up where I am I can see the whole valley. The 'fort' must have been an observation post.

I make my way through the ruins to the section with a roof, where we can shelter from the sun. I share some water with Prince, who slumps at my side and sighs with weariness. The trek has taken a lot out of him. I spot a rusting helmet poking out of some rubble and tug it free. It's a Russian helmet. Not far from it is an insect-ravaged payroll book, with entries written in Russian. The battle that destroyed the outpost must have happened more than thirty years ago, after the Soviet Union invaded the country. That's how long the locals have had to put up with foreign soldiers on their soil.

Leafing through the payroll book, looking at the numbers, I wonder who it had belonged to. Was he back in Moscow, now middle-aged and still bewildered that the huge Russian forces had been humbled by poorly armed locals? Or had he been killed here in this foreign land? In my short time in Afghanistan I've come to see death in war as a matter of chance. Why did one man like Casey die and not me? It didn't take me long to discover that there are two sorts of soldiers, those who have absolute confidence they will live and the others who are resigned to the idea that they will die. Both are wrong. Chance dictates everything. On one patrol I was sitting in the rear of a Bushmaster, shooting the breeze with a lieutenant who was on his second tour. He was saying something about how his girlfriend hated his taste in music when he slapped the side of his head, as if squashing a mosquito, and slumped over me. Somehow, and from somewhere, a stray bullet had sought him out; found him but not me. Chance. Death was like a lottery. It made no sense at all. Chance determined everything in war – even Casey said that.

I look at my map. We have covered the ground I wanted to achieve today. If we keep up this pace then we will make it back to base in four more days. I try to concentrate on staying awake but find I can't stop from yawning. Prince is snoring softly. I want to guard us both but I'm unable to stop my eyelids from closing and I can feel I am falling into a deep sleep.

5

When I wake up it's late in the afternoon. Even in the shade of the shattered roof the heat is almost unbearable. Prince is lying on his side, tongue lolling out. There's little water left in my canteen. I sip enough to quench my thirst and find it's warm. I clean the inside of the helmet and pour a few mouthfuls of water into it for Prince, who laps up every last drop. Once we're on the move again we'll have to find more.

While I'm waiting for evening I walk to the ruined walls and peer down into the valley. I can see figures in the poppy fields, either side of the river. There also seems to be a small orchard on the far bank. It's probably best to stay on the western side where the hills are less steep.

Back in the shade I chew some gum to try and produce saliva into my dry mouth. Prince sniffs around the shadows, looking for food. I whistle to him but he doesn't react. I just hope that he'll get back his hearing as I did.

I hear a noise above me and look up through a ragged hole in the roof at the clear sky. A Black Hawk helicopter swoops low and passes quickly overhead before I can attract the pilot's attention. It flies on in the direction of our rescue raid. The pilot will spot the remains of the second chopper and see that no one has survived. I only hope that they can at least recover Casey's body and give him a proper burial. By now his girlfriend, Penny, will have been told that he is dead or missing. She will be inconsolable. They were going to be married once Casey had finished his tour. He'd spend hours at night on Skype talking to her back in Australia, Prince snoozing at his feet. The others and I would tease him about it, but he'd reply, *At least I've got a girlfriend, which is more than most of you wankers have.*

I'm thinking about Casey and Penny when it strikes me for the first time that people back home in Australia will also believe I'm dead. My father will have been told by now – I have no idea how he will deal with it. He begged me not to sign up, not to go to Afghanistan. *But look at the positive side of things – I've got you,* I say to Prince, running my fingers through his fur looking for ticks as I saw Casey do. He twists his head at an angle as if trying to understand me. He knows he's being talked to, but hears nothing. *Poor Prince, poor boy,* I say, stroking him.

He turns away on noticing something out in the glare. Two scorpions, their barbed tails raised in readiness, are stalking a brown lizard sunning itself on a rock. One jumps at the lizard and stings it, while the other does the same. The lizard shivers and goes still. The scorpions turn on each other, quarrelling over the dead lizard. They'll keep on fighting, even if that means they both die. The way Prince is staring at them it seems that he too understands that they're in a dance of death. *I know*, I say to him, *it's pointless, like this war. If the Taliban aren't fighting us, they're killing fellow Afghans. To survive here, you have to kill; to fight is to survive. It's as basic and primitive as those two scorpions, old boy.*

I laugh as Prince frowns at me, as if he's puzzling over this too. I didn't understand how Casey could talk to his dog as if it were a human, but now I know. It's as if he *feels* what I am saying. As Casey used to say, *The great thing about dogs is that they don't answer back, so you can talk to them to your heart's content.*

The rusting artillery shells shine in the glare. It's a reminder that the Russians couldn't win here and neither will we. Soon the desert will claim even the ruins and they'll disappear into the baking earth as if they had never existed.

The sun is setting. I find myself smiling at Prince,

who is looking worried, as if concerned by my brooding. *What are your deep thoughts about the matter, my black prince?* He tilts his head as if trying to figure out what I'm yabbering on about. Some insects have settled on his flank, attracted to the raw wound. I wipe them away and then scratch his throat. His eyes close in bliss. He doesn't complain, he's brave, stoic and loyal and yet has no idea that he's in a war.

It reminds me that those back at the base will think Prince is also dead. I remember when an army dog died in an explosion and at the memorial service his food bowl was placed upside-down next to his kennel. It was the symbol that a dog had been killed. The sight of the upturned bowl was too much for the handler, who moved away to sit by himself at the end of the compound, among the truck parts and boxes, where he wept like a baby. Now I understand his grief. *We're going to get back together*, I say as he licks my hand, wanting me to continue scratching his throat. *We're a team, OK?*

Shadows, which as usual seem darker and deeper than those in Australia, are beginning to creep across the ruins as the sun sinks quickly. I stand up and as I prepare, I notice that the two scorpions are dead, the lizard not far from them, stiff and shrunken to a tiny piece of meat in the heat.

The farmers have returned to their village as we make our way down to the stream, passing through a field of poppies. It's colder now. The moon is rising and the light shines on some strange lumps scattered on the ground. I bend over them and realise I'm standing in a watermelon patch. I cut off a hunk of watermelon and eat it. How delicious it is; fresh and filled with sugary water, it soothes my dry mouth and lips and stops my stomach from rumbling. We'll have to find water and some real food soon, though, or we won't have the energy for the trek.

The next stop will be to get some water and then we'll head south, bypassing a village. Prince trots ahead of me. That's what I like about him – his independence and his sense that he is any man's equal. As we move through long grass and stunted trees, I notice him sniffing the ground with increasing urgency. Then he breaks into a run. *Prince, stop!* I call, but he's unable to hear me. He changes direction and I see he is chasing after something. He breaks free of the grass and closes in on a small animal, like a hare. They cross the stubble of a harvested maize field and I can see their two silhouettes as Prince gains on his prey. Unlike a lot of other dogs, Prince never barks when hunting. There's no tell-tale sign of excitement: his is a relentless and silent pursuit.

There's a movement to my right. For a moment I think it's a scarecrow quivering in the night wind, then I realise it's a man. He pauses on spotting me and then sets off at high speed. I can't raise my voice or shoot him because I don't want to wake the village but I have to stop him before he can warn anyone. I chase after him, slowly gaining but he's too far ahead for me to catch him. My army boots make running across the fields hard going, it's as if they're made of concrete. I glance over my left shoulder to see where Prince is. He's rounding in on the animal, causing it to double back in fear. In turning to bring it down, Prince sees me chasing after the Afghan and stops in his tracks.

He pauses as if deciding between the prey and me and, sizing up the situation, changes direction and starts to chase after the man. He passes me in that effortless lope of his and silently gains on the Afghan, who spins around, only to see Prince leaping at him. The man yelps in shock and stumbles to the ground. Prince clamps his jaw on the man's arm to stop him from getting away. Terrified, he pleads in a wild babble, trying to back away on his bum from the dog. *Stop, Prince. No more*, I order when I catch up to him, but he can't hear so I have to tap him on the neck and motion him to let go of the arm which he does and obediently sits down not far away, his attention focused on the man, whose eyes, caught in the moonlight, are sparkling with fear.

I mime to him to put his hands behind his head, which he does. His eyes switch back and forth between the rifle barrel pointing down at him and the dog. He doesn't look like a Taliban soldier; his straggly beard, creased face and rough clothes mean he's probably a farmer. But why was he was out in the fields at this time? I know Afghans don't like the night. Maybe he's been out hunting? But he has no weapon. I have a few basic words of Pashto and use some on him, telling him not to move or I'll kill him. He doesn't seem to understand what I'm saying to him, either because he's so frightened or because he's from another ethnic group that speaks a different language. There's no way I can kill an unarmed citizen. The problem is that if I free him, it's certain he'll raise the alarm about us.

His head swivels towards the river. Prince has seen something too and jumps up, staring in the same direction. I see a figure running along the river's edge, heading towards the village. He's wearing only a light white shift and is barefoot. When he passes from the shadows into the moonlight I notice he's only a boy, maybe a teenager. Prince glances at up at me, ready to obey an order to chase after him but there's no point. I have little idea of what to do with the man at my feet, let alone two captives. What's certain is that it won't be long before the youngster wakes up the village. My heart's racing; my mind is a blur – I have to make a decision as soon as possible.

I motion the Afghan to lie face down in the stubble. He obediently rolls onto his stomach. I yank off his trousers and use them to tie his hands behind his back. Then I press the rifle barrel against his neck, telling him to stay still and be quiet until we've gone. He may not know any English but the threat of being shot is a universal language and he'll heed my warning – at least for a while.

There's nothing I can do about the boy. Soon the village will be out searching for an enemy soldier and his dog, so it's crucial we put as much distance as possible between us and them.

Prince looks up at me as if wanting to know what will happen next. The sweat of effort and fear drips into my eyes. I hear the boy yelling out as he approaches the village. Some lights go on.

6

It's best to return to the observation post rather than risking being seen out in the open. The moonlight is as bright as a searchlight. By the time we reach the ruins, my uniform is heavy with sweat and I'm panting with effort. Prince seems to know the dangerous situation we're in. The way he's sticking close and sometimes looking up at me with that familiar frown of his, it's as if he senses my urgency.

It takes me some time to recover. I sit on a pile of rocks that was once a wall and gaze down on the barren hills that lead up to the observation post. It's the best position from which to see if anyone is following us. Thin white lines move around in the darkness below. It takes me some time to realise that they are torchlights – it must be the villagers looking for us. Prince sits a few metres from me, looking in the same direction. I feel an intense respect for him. The way he helped me out without me even ordering him to was extraordinary.

I don't know if he's forgotten Casey, but he seems to have decided that we're a team.

We'll have to stay in the ruins, then set out tomorrow night and try to catch up on the time we've lost. I pick up my canteen and take a sip, only to realise there's no water left. I didn't have time to fill it up. It's going to be difficult to sit out the heat of the day unless we can find some. Prince needs it more than I do; dogs suffer more from the heat than humans. I learned on patrol that the sniffer dogs can only work for about twenty minutes without rest and water.

I try not to doze off. Because the Taliban wear black it'll be easy for them to avoid being seen once the moon drops behind the mountains. Casey said the Russians called their Afghan enemy *dukhi* or ghosts, and I can understand that. On patrol I've spotted Taliban soldiers only to have them vanish in front of me as if they never existed.

Towards dawn I wake up in the middle of a nightmare of the Taliban chasing Prince and me across boiling earth so hot that it burns through my boots and sears his paws. The morning sun is beginning to pour down on the outpost. I stand up and stretch my limbs only to realise that I'm alone. Prince has gone. I call out his name, then remember he is deaf. A terrible dread possesses me. I run through the ruins of the fort.

Then, just when I think he may have wandered off into the desert to look for Casey, I see him standing in the shadow of an overhanging rock at the rear of the fort. He's staring intently at some object. I run to him and he glances up at me with a frown of concentration and then back at a piece of rusted tin about two metres square on the ground weighed down by large rocks. *What is it, Prince?* His stumpy tail wiggles with excitement. I pull him back, afraid there may be snakes or scorpions under the tin sheet. After removing the rocks, I carefully lift up the piece of tin with the barrel of my rifle. There's a round hole about a metre across. I peer into it and hear Prince next to me sniffing loudly. The inside lining of the hole is reinforced with bricks. I can make out nothing in the pitch blackness. I drop a stone into it and after a second or two I hear a faint splash. *Prince, you're brilliant!* I cry out in relief and laugh as he prances around the hole, eager to get at the water.

It's impossible to reach to touch the water, so I grab the helmet and search for string or a rope, but there's nothing. I take off my shirt and tie one sleeve to the chinstrap and, holding on to the other sleeve, lower the helmet into the well. Just when I think the sleeves aren't long enough, I hear a hard splash as it hits the water. I spend an agonising time trying to tilt the helmet enough so that water will flow into it. Once

I've done that I carefully lift it up out of the well. Prince steps forward to drink but I push him away. He seems annoyed and his body goes rigid, as if wanting to fight me for it. I motion him to be calm. *It's OK, boy, I just want to make sure.*

I put some of the water on my dry lips. It's cool and slightly brackish, but seems good enough to drink. Prince trembles with impatience, he's even more thirsty than I thought. Convinced it's fine to drink, I place the helmet on the ground in front of him and he laps up the water greedily. I pat him as he drinks, telling him over and over, *Good boy, good boy . . . who's the clever devil now?* I dip the helmet into the well several more times until the both of us have drunk our fill. I put my soaking wet shirt back on. The damp coolness is a relief. The shirt dries in a few minutes but I feel refreshed. *You've saved my bacon again*, I say to Prince. He seems to shrug away my praise and heads off, sniffing his way through the ruins. I started out fearing he would be a burden and now I don't think I could make it back without him.

I walk to the remains of the stone fence and perch where I have a one-eighty-degree view. I scan the slopes and escarpments for signs of life. But there are none. I'm relieved and not a little puzzled; perhaps the village hasn't reported our presence to the Taliban, or maybe it doesn't consider us important enough to chase. I watch the tiny people in the valley, toiling under the harsh sun. In a nearby paddock, two dozen or so small figures run back and forth in a helter-skelter fashion. Their movements don't make sense – and then I figure it out; they're playing soccer.

I'm about to return to the shade when I glimpse a movement to my far right. Three armed men in black are advancing quickly and with purpose towards the fort. There's no doubt they're after us. We don't have much time. I grab Prince and motion him to follow me out of the ruins.

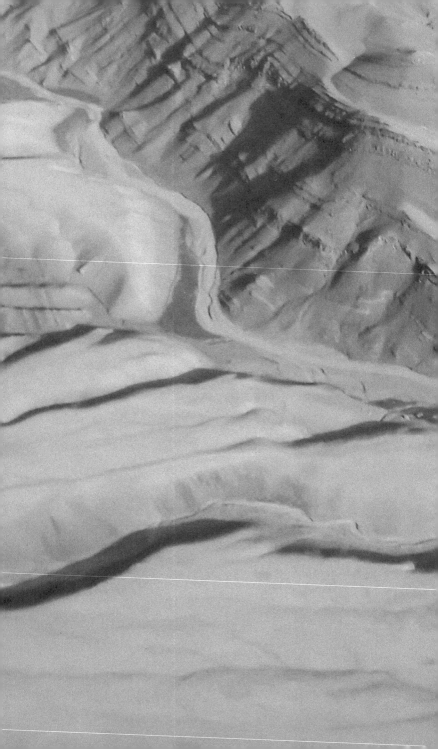

7

There's nowhere to hide. The air is thin and hot and my lips are cracked. I have to keep careful watch on Prince in this furnace. He keeps pace with me and I take frequent rests. Even so, he's walking more slowly and his tongue hangs out. I get him to sit, and pour water from my canteen down his throat. Then he lies on the dirt and licks his paws. I'm horrified by how blistered they are from the hot stones and earth.

It only gets worse when I notice three black dots following us across the ridges. Prince is breathing heavily. I have to find shelter soon or he'll die. I brush my hand back and forth across his back, calming him. There's no way he can survive several more hours in these terrible conditions. All we can do is to keep moving in the hope we'll find a hiding place soon.

I take a sip of the warm water and steel myself for the next section. Prince sets off with me, but walking slowly and gingerly, as if his paws hurt each step. I want to hurry but I have to keep to his pace. I wish he could hear, so I could urge him on. I keep patting him, hoping my touch is reassuring him.

Climbing a hill is painful – we're both gutted with the heat and effort. At the top I look at what is in store for us. It's a wasteland. I'm feeling dizzy from the searing heat and the glare. Prince stops and licks one of his damaged paws. I'm wondering if we should somehow double back and return to the fort again, just to seek shade, when I see a cluster of large rocks at the foot of a hill. It's just after midday and the sun is travelling west; perhaps we can find some shade on the eastern side of the rocks.

We have to stop frequently for Prince to gather his strength. His eyes are glazed with the heat and pain and I don't think we'll make it, but after an hour or so we finally reach the shelter of the rocks. The main one is the size of a door, and it casts a hard black shadow on the cracked earth. The shade is a relief. Prince lies on his stomach, his body heaving as he recovers from the ordeal. The temperature may still be high but resting here is much safer than being exposed, and my eyes no longer have to deal with the intense white glare that bounces off the earth and stones. I give Prince more water, leaving a couple of sips for myself. The water is as hot as a cup of tea but I don't care. I'm grateful to Prince for having found the well because we surely would have died from thirst without it. I keep watch over him, feeling helpless – there's very little more I can do. Gradually his breathing becomes regular and he's relaxed enough to doze. My face is hot and flushed and I feel blisters on my unshaven cheeks. We'll wait until dusk before setting off again. In the meantime I keep an eye open for the Taliban and study my map. We've been going south-west, but it's time to head south-east.

I'm working out how long it will take us to reach the river when I hear voices. I drop the map and peek around the rock. The three Taliban are moving around the side of a hill, heading towards us. I hear Prince sniffing the air. He's smelt them and the hair stands up along his spine. He growls softly. I touch his head to quieten him and make him sit, then I loosen the safety catch on my rifle. The voices become louder as though they are having a conversation. I realise I am not breathing and tell myself to breathe in and out to calm myself. My heart is beating hard. I'll have to shoot them first before they spot us. I don't dare look out to see where they are until I am ready to fire. I can hear their voices clearly now. They seem to be chatting about something that amuses them, because one of them laughs. They sound as though they're only ten metres from me. A two-way radio crackles into life. Out of the corner of my eye I see Prince stand, and as his nose sniffs, his lips quiver and his tongue flicks in and out as if he is tasting the very air itself. I know this sign, I've seen it on patrol. He's about to attack. As he steps forward, I grab his collar. He whips around, ready to turn on me. I motion him to sit. He stares at me as if irritated that I am stopping him.

One of the men answers the call and he sounds angry. Not even knowing the language, I can tell he's swearing. Then there's silence. I strain to hear if they're moving. They talk as if debating among themselves what to do about the call. My hands are so slippery with sweat that I have to rub them dry on my trousers. I hear them set off again and I hold my finger against the trigger, deciding to take the middle Taliban first. It will confuse the other two for a moment and I'll be able to get more shots in. Instead of coming closer, their voices fade away. I peer around the rock and see them trudging back up the hill. Relief floods through me and the tension drains away. *That was close, eh, Prince?* He stares at me, frowning, as if to say, *What was that all about? I could have taken them myself.*

The shadows grow longer and as the sun sets I take another look at Prince. He trembles when I touch his sore feet. At least the earth will be cool when we finally move out. We seem to have shaken off the Taliban for the time being. Perhaps they were ordered on another mission. The bright orange sun drops below the horizon with a suddenness that is peculiar to this country, and the moon, like a gigantic white hole tunnelling into the inky blackness, looms up from behind the distant mountains. It's time to go. The moon's silver light will make it easy for us to find our way along the contours of the slopes.

Nearing the river, we find ourselves in an orchard of trees twisted into weird shapes. I recognise the fruit as pomegranates. I pluck three, the size of apples, while Prince hurries to the river and jumps into it, standing in the water up to his chest; no doubt the water eases the pain of his sore pads. I fill my canteen and almost drink it dry before filling it up again. I sit down on the bank and cut open the pomegranates with my knife, removing the pulp and enjoying the tart juice and sugary seeds. The moon is huge, as if it were close enough to touch. Everything seems peaceful. I eat the pomegranates but know that what we need is meat. Prince can't make it back home without protein, and the fruit won't be enough for me either. If we can't find meat in the next day or so, then we'll have to risk stealing a village sheep or goat.

Prince sits in the water, the reflected moonlight

making him look as if his fur is covered in frost. What is called a river in Afghanistan would only be a creek back in Australia. Emerald Creek runs behind my family's house and during her last summer my mother would sit in the shallow eddies at night, cooling off, as Prince is doing. She'd sit in the water for hours in her blue bikini staring at the top of the burning mountain, which glowed red in the darkness. Something was happening to her body. She had begun to lose weight and the doctors had no idea what was the cause. Some thought it might have been the result of poisonous gases escaping from the cracks in the earth as the underground coal burned. Even if that was true, she didn't want to leave the town where she had been born.

As she grew more ill she'd gaze for hours out the windows, as if hankering for something in the beyond. She stopped cooking dinner, so Dad or I did it, only we were woeful chefs and we mostly ate canned food. Mum would pick at her meal but she seemed so preoccupied that she cared nothing for food, it was as if she thought she could survive on air alone. She grew thinner, lived in her dressing gown, went barefoot most of the time. Dad bought her a pair of scarlet slippers so her feet would be warm. *Just click them together and you'll be back in Kansas,* he said to her, making a joke out of her favourite film, *The Wizard of Oz*. During winter, when it was snowing and too cold to go outside, she'd stand in the living room, staring at her feet and snapping her heels together as she tried to make her soft slippers click.

I was only eleven at the time but I knew that something was deeply wrong and that there was no cure for whatever was making her ill. When spring came she'd stand on the back verandah and gaze at Emerald Creek as it swelled with melting snow; or she'd close her eyes, trying to click her slippers together, and then on opening them she'd look around, grimacing with disappointment that she wasn't where she wanted to be. She showed no interest in what Dad and I said to her and she stopped talking altogether, as if it were too much effort to listen or to speak. She didn't like being touched but she'd allow me or Dad to comb her long blonde hair, something she had always enjoyed. We'd do it because it relaxed her and she'd smile to herself as if at some secret joke. Both Dad and I pretended not to smell the whisky or wine on her breath.

The feeling in the house was so awful, so filled with my mother's silence and my father's sighs, that when not at school I'd try to spend as much time as possible outdoors, hunting with Casey or exploring the rusting mining machinery scattered across the mountain. The mine was supposed to re-open when a way was found to the stop the underground coal burning. There had been a mysterious explosion deep in a tunnel that caused a fire which couldn't be put out. Because of that the mine was too dangerous to work in and had to close.

The town was nicknamed Burning Mountain. The grass withered and the trees caught fire, so that the area around the mine became a steaming desert. Most of the locals had something to do with the mine, whether as workers or people married to miners, as office staff or techies like my father, the chief engineer. If the mine had been at the bottom of a valley the creek could have been diverted, with the water flooding the tunnels to put out the fires, but as it was at the top of a hill it was impossible to do that. My father was one of the few men kept on by the mine owners in the hope that a solution would be found, but when he stopped going to his office because there was nothing to do, he seemed resigned to the mine never re-opening.

Late one morning Dad looked in on Mum only to see her dead on top of the bedclothes, wearing her dressing gown and red slippers, with the window wide open and the room freezing cold. After the funeral, Dad kept even more to himself. We'd eat our baked beans or sausages in silence. He'd sit on the front verandah at night, drinking whisky, staring into the night, as if he were waiting for Mum to come back. He didn't seem to notice me. Sometimes he'd roast a rabbit or wallaby I'd shot when I was out hunting with Casey. One dinner he was eating a rabbit leg when he suddenly spat out a bullet. He paused to look at it on the side of his plate and laughed. It was the first time he had laughed since the funeral. *Thank goodness it wasn't grapeshot!* I laughed too, just out of pleasure at seeing him happy for a moment. Most times he ate and slept by himself in the study. When Casey's family found out about my home life they'd have me around to dinner most nights. At first it was awkward but soon Casey was treating me like his younger brother. Sometimes I slept over but if I didn't, I'd go home and, if I saw a light under the study door, I'd knock and open the door, poke my head in and say goodnight. If Dad were not too drunk or depressed he'd say he loved me and he'd get better. *That's a promise, son.*

At school I was the class clown. At home I was lonely and asked for a Labrador like the one Casey had, but dad wouldn't allow it. On one occasion when I asked him, his face twisted in a fury as if he wanted to throttle me. I backed away. He must have seen my fear because his face softened. *I'm sorry, son, I'm bad luck. Everything I touch turns to dust. My job, your beautiful mother. The dog would only die. I'm a curse. I'm bad luck.* I could see in his tortured eyes that he fully believed this, because it struck me that he hadn't touched me since my mother died.

I remember her look of relief when she sat cooling off in the water in the moonlight; now, sitting in the creek, Prince has the same expression. He notices me looking at him and he stares back at me with the confidence of an equal. Never having had a dog of my own, I'm beginning to understand Casey's love for him. *It's us two against the Taliban, mate.* He must realise I said something to him because he walks out of the river and, after a quick shake, drying him but wetting me, he sits down at my feet. *Good boy, good boy, we're going to get back and you can have your special ball to play with*, I whisper, and he licks my hand.

8

I pack a few pomegranates in my kit and we set out to climb the steep hills, zigzagging our way up and down, using the goat and sheep tracks. The air is cool and we're making good time. It's only when dawn comes and I'm looking for a village to raid for food that I'm stunned by the realisation that the valley we are supposed to be entering is not there.

In front of us is a series of steep, sharp ridges. I'm bewildered; somehow I made a wrong turning during the night. I have no idea where we are. I study the map and try to orientate myself. It's nigh on impossible. The map is vague about the areas to the south-east of the valley, showing hills and mountains but not names or distances. That must be where I am now. I have no idea how far we have travelled from the valley I want. It could be kilometres – but how many? How could I be so stupid? We're lost. I slump down on the ground in despair.

I feel Prince staring at me. He seems sad like me. It's then I remember Casey telling me that dogs are sensitive to their handler's emotions. If you're having a bad day, the dog is going to have a bad day. I glance at him and then away, feeling guilty. This is no good. I have to convince him I know where we are. I jump up, pretending enthusiasm. *There's no need to look at me that way, my Black Prince, I'm completely on top of things. Now to nick a sheep.* His eyes immediately brighten. There's a movement above us and looking at the clear blue sky, I notice what looks like a vulture, or maybe it's an eagle, drifting around in circles in the hot air currents. Perhaps because it's so high up it can see the whole countryside and knows we're lost and alone and is waiting for us to die.

The sight of the predator makes me determined to keep moving. We head west, down a steep incline and across a ridge. The sun is rising and we need shelter. On top of the ridge I try to find some sort of landmark that might be on the map, but there's none. The only thing to do is to double back to where the valley should be. I give Prince a drink of water and I'm about to have a sip of it myself when I see what looks like a man-made structure to the south- east, just beyond another, smaller ridge. It's nestled in a spot between hills, like a small village or an observation fort like the one we stayed in. The important thing is that if it's empty it can be our refuge for the day, and maybe we'll find some food there before we head in the right direction again. I nod to a frowning Prince as if to say, *I know what I'm doing, mate.*

It takes us nearly two hours to reach the next ridge because for Prince each step of his raw pads on the hot earth is painful. Just in case the place is occupied, I crawl to the crest. Prince crawls on his belly beside me, as he's been taught. The buildings are surrounded by mud walls, with a clump of trees in the main yard. The front gates are open and I can't see anything moving; human or animal. The sun is beating down on us so relentlessly that my sweat evaporates on my skin in seconds.

There's no other alternative. As we walk down the slope I occasionally stop to make sure no one is in the compound. I listen but can hear nothing, only my heavy breathing and Prince's panting. When we're within a hundred metres I notice dozens of tyre marks and foot-prints leading out of the compound. The wind hasn't blown them away so they must have been made not so long ago. My heart begins to thump and a queasy feeling takes hold of me. Just how recent are they? And is anyone still inside? I clutch my rifle tightly, take a deep breath and we go through the open gates. There's a small pond near the four poplar trees in the far corner and a vegetable garden with spades and forks scattered across it and nearby an upended wheelbarrow as if the gardeners have left in a hurry.

The signs of an exodus give me the jitters. Why have these people fled so quickly and will they be coming back? Prince glances up at me. He's puzzled too. I hear a noise and spin around, but it's only the flapping of a plastic sheet covering one of the windows. I don't know how much time we've got but we have to hurry. The first thing is to get some food; for Prince, preferably meat. We cross the compound yard to a doorway. It's covered in a dark blue cloth. I pull it open and peer inside. My eyes take a few moments to grow used to the dim light, then I make out that the shapes on the floor are mattresses, maybe up to a dozen of them.

We move on to the next door. It's wooden and un-locked. I push it open, step inside and reel at the stink of sweetness and decay. There is the sharp odour of marijuana. Attached to the far wall are rows of shelves covered in dried poppy plants. Stacked along the wall are two-hundred-litre drums. I look inside one and see kilos of brown sludge. I recognise the smell. On the far benches is distilling equipment – glass tubes, bottles of chemicals, lumps of semi-processed heroin and sacks of opium. I've seen set-ups like this before. It's a heroin production laboratory. And a big one by the looks of it.

I'm about to step back into the sunshine when I hear a squeaky child's voice, speaking in English. *Rifle on the ground and put your hands up!* I turn and see a fleeting movement in the three large piles of marijuana plants. Then everything is still for a moment before a figure comes into the light, with dried hemp and twigs stuck to her clothes. She's about a metre tall, wearing a brown burqa with the face grille torn away and holding a revolver in both hands, which she's pointing at me. I'm so surprised to see her that I can only stare at her like an idiot. *The rifle!* she demands. I put it on one of the workbenches. I hear Prince come in. *I kill you first and then the dog.* She aims the pistol at Prince, who goes still, tensing his body. His eyes, like two laser beams, focus on her throat and his lips begin to tremble as if he's muttering to himself – I know what that means. *Stay, stay Prince.* He doesn't hear me and I have to tap him on the flank and let him know I don't want him to attack her. *Now the gun!* she orders, and I place the Glock next to the rifle.

The girl laughs and steps closer. The revolver seems enormous in her tiny hands. She points it at Prince. *What happens if I kill your dog?* I don't say anything. Her English has a strong American accent. The sunlight pours into the room and catches her eyes, the only part of her body visible. They are an unhealthy red

with yellow rings. *Do you know where my guys went?*
I shake my head. *Woke up before, and they'd hit the
road. Big surprise. Didn't tell me.* She peers up at me.
You're not American?

No, I'm Australian.

An Aussie?

Yes.

You're a long way from home, buddy.

It's as I meet her gaze that I notice she has lines
around her eyes, like a middle-aged person. I glance
at her tiny hands; they're wrinkled like those of an
adult. Prince sits at my side waiting for my command.
His head is bent forward and he's sniffing the girl as if
trying to figure out who's under the burqa. She takes
a few careful steps backwards. *Hey, pal, control that
mutt or I'll shoot its head off.*

I pull Prince back, patting him on the neck, letting
him know I'm in control and to keep calm.

So watcha doin' here, Aussie?

Just passing by.

Out here? What are you – some kind of bozo?
I repeat my question. Here? Why?

Food.

She makes a rough, loud sound, as if she's trying
to clear her throat of something dangerous and coughs
loudly. *Ack! Ack!*

I jump, it's so strange and unexpected. The girl giggles at my reaction. *Ack! Ack!* she coughs again. I catch Prince looking at me, wondering why I reacted the way I did, because, of course, he's heard nothing. The girl laughs. *You know, when my guys return, they're gonna pat me on the back. I got me a prisoner and his dirty dog. I'll get respect.*

She looks around the room. *Kinda stinks, doesn't it? But you get used to it. Turn around . . . and keep your mitts up!*

I don't like turning my back on her but do as I'm told. *The same with your mutt – I don't like the way he's staring at me.*

He's deaf. He can't hear.

She breaks into her *Ack! Ack!* cry and follows it up with a tinny laugh as if she's enjoying making me uncomfortable. I hear her grunt with effort behind me. *It gets damn hot in this.* Something soft falls onto the floorboards. *Hey, Aussie, get a load of this.* I turn around and I'm astonished by what I see. This is no girl pointing a gun at me; it's a boy wearing dirty white runners, bright red shorts, blue suspenders to hold them up, and a pink T-shirt with a cute child's face, big saucer eyes and the words *Mother's Little Helper* printed across the image.

He's tiny. His legs are thin as sticks, though his face

is that of an adult. Without the burqa he looks naked, like a turtle without its shell. Either he's a dwarf or a midget. *Yeah, I know*, he says, smiling slyly, *I am not quite like a man. I am a tiny man. But a man all the same, and I can kill you as easily as any normal guy.* He laughs again, and bursts into the weird strangled cry of *Ack! Ack!*

He holds the revolver in one hand and rubs his forehead with the other as if he has forgotten something. *I don't know where it is*, the tiny man finally says, as if he were answering a question of mine. He surveys the room and shakes his head, as if appalled by what he sees. *Let's get out of here, too many temptations, buddy.*

He prods me in the back with his gun and ushers me out, saying, *Remember, Aussie, I could blow a hole as big as a fist in your back.* We cross the dirt courtyard to another room, with no door, just a grey blanket covering it. He motions with his gun for me to go inside. Prince comes in with me. Barely the size of a toilet, the room smells of stale sweat and dirty clothes. *A dump I call home*, the squeaky voice behind me says. *There it is!* he cries, brushing past me and picking up a large, slim paperback. He hugs it to his chest with one arm and smacks his lips. *I feel thirsty.*

We walk back across the compound to another doorway. The room inside has a window, so it isn't as dark as the others. Thick oriental rugs, pillows and cushions are scattered on the floor; all coloured blue, red, yellow and green. The walls are hung with ruby-red velvet drapes. It's a living room and reception area. There's another room off to the side, which looks like a kitchen. *You're worth more to me alive than dead*, he says, tugging at my sleeve and looking up at me with his sly smile. He's enjoying making me feel uneasy. Suddenly he cries out, *Get him away!* and tumbles backwards. Prince must have accidentally touched him. The revolver drops from his hand when he lands. If I'd been closer I could have made a jump for it, but he knows what I'm thinking and, still on his back, grabs the gun and points it up at me. *If that devil touches me one more time, buster, I'm gonna put a bullet through his head.*

He scrambles to his feet and grinds his teeth, agitated or maybe embarrassed by his outburst. He stares at Prince with undisguised loathing. He clutches his gun tightly as if debating whether to shoot him or not. I step between him and Prince. *By the time you shoot him I'd have jumped you*, I warn. He can see that I mean it.

Get him outside. Now!

Prince has no idea what is happening. Under the watchful eye of the midget, I motion Prince to stay outside near the doorway. The midget points me into the next room. It's like most Afghan kitchens: basic – with a gas-cylinder stove, a small kerosene fridge, sacks of food and cans of cooking oil. Unwashed plates and food are scattered on a wooden bench as if the preparations for a meal have been interrupted. *Ah, raisins*, he says, scoffing down a handful he takes from a bowl. He chews them hungrily, brown juice running down the sides of his mouth. He doesn't offer me any but watches me carefully as he eats. Then he picks at the raisins stuck between his teeth and asks me what I'm doing here.

I was on a patrol when I got lost.

He smiles, as if he doesn't believe me. *When my boys come back, they'll get the right answer. Name?*

Corporal Mark Hollis.

A lousy corporal. When I was with the Americans I only mixed with officers. I'm Ghulam. Nice to meet you, Corporal Hollis.

I can't help but smile, it sounds as if he is imitating an English gentleman. *Nice to meet you, Ghulam.*

Afghans are very hospitable people. We look after our guests. Hey, what's your father's name?

In my short time on tour I've learned that this is an important question in Afghanistan. They always want to know your father's name, who he was or is, where he fits into society and what kind of family you come from. *My father's name is Thomas Hollis, he's a mining engineer. We live in the mountains. My mother is dead. I am the only child.*

Ghulum ponders the information. *I think my mother and father are dead. My foster father is Captain Duncan. I think I am an only child too.*

The introductions reduce the tension and he passes me the bowl. I take out a handful of raisins and begin to eat them. *I'm fattening you up, Corporal.* He throws me a hunk of flat bread. *Be my guest.* I tear off a piece and chew it.

He eats his bread as he sizes me up. He says something but because his mouth is full I don't understand a word. When he realises, he repeats it. *Americans have all the food you care to eat. That's why most are big like elephants, especially those black dudes. This group of clowns here eat crappy food. You never go hungry with the Americans.*

He sighs and chews some more, his mouth bulging with bread. Something is nagging him. *You guys are rich like Americans, aren't you? I mean, we're poor compared to you.*

Yes. I've never seen so many poor people in my life.

He nods in silent agreement. His accent and ease in speaking American English is impressive compared to the lousy English of most Afghans. I decide to flatter him. *How did you learn such great English?*

It works; he smiles with pleasure, almost preening. Then he tells me about his background. Because of his disability his parents put him in an orphanage. He was six years old when the building was destroyed by a wayward American rocket. He was found in the rubble by a medical officer who carried him to the American compound in Kabul. The Americans took a shine to him and he became their mascot. He picked up English easily and knew how to, as he said, *act the goat*. He kept on mentioning a Captain Duncan whom he was very close to. *He showed me things*, he said mysteriously. When the Captain finished his tour and returned home, Ghulum was devastated. He had become such a fixture at the compound that he was taken for granted. He no longer seemed special. Depressed and lonely, he started using heroin, not caring if he lived or died. One day while he was walking down a side street after scoring, a car stopped beside him and a man jumped out of the passenger seat and grabbed him. He was driven out of Kabul and after a journey of several hours ended up in a village where Taliban soldiers were holed up. Their leader had seen Ghulum in the streets a few weeks before. Like the Americans he wanted the midget as his mascot and good-luck charm.

Ghulum taps his head saying, *The guy was nuts,*

I had to shave his whole body 'cos he thought that hairs on his body was a sign he was an ape, not a true human. I went through hundreds of razors, I mean, man, his back was like fur. The memory of shaving the man's back causes him to act out a comical shiver, which makes me smile.

All told, he has been with the Americans for eight years and with the Taliban for four. It's only when I start to add up the years that I realise he is younger than I thought, perhaps eighteen years old, like me. After his kidnapper died in a drone attack on his car, Ghulum remained with the Taliban. Some of them teased him and would dress him as a girl or throw him around the compound like a football. But they kept him because their revered leader had adored him.

After telling me his story he lapses into silence for a time, standing in the kitchen, staring vacantly at the floor as if he is trying to make sense of his life. Dressed the way he is, he looks like a lost child. I'm aware I could jump him but I don't. I'm still trying to come to terms with how weird this is. I feel like pinching myself just to make sure I'm not dreaming. He lifts his head and groans softly, as if all he understood of his past was that he was always at the mercy of someone else, whether it be his parents, the Americans or the Taliban. *You been to Kabul?* he asks. I nod. *The big*

city is where I belong, man, not in the badlands here.
His face brightens with remembered pleasure. *Oh boy,
one day Captain Duncan and me go to this really big
boss guy. His lift was made out of gold, man! All the
furniture was leather. Ceilings shiny with gilt, parquet
floors and statues of men and women half undressed,
and they had these green, pink and blue lights shining
on them. And get this, dude, a television operated by
a voice. I spoke to it and told it to turn on and it did,
man. It did. You like Kabul, dude? Course you would.
Ever do ten-pin bowling there?*

Didn't know you could.

*I mixed with the big boys, you didn't. The Yanks
have got a couple of really good bowling alleys. Jeez,
and their food. Not nuts and raisins like this dump.
Cheeseburgers. Steaks as big as your head. Fajitas.
Ever taste fajitas?*

I shake my head.

Well, you would if you had it. Kabul . . . he says
softly. *Kabul's my aim, man. I'm gonna get back there.
I'm gonna go bowling and eat icecream in Kabul.
Kabul . . .* His voice trails off, his eyes gleaming as if he
has been transported back there and is experiencing it
just as intensely as the first time.

He looks at the kitchen and sighs at the contrast.
Ack! Ack! he cries and orders me into the living room.

I say that Prince is starving and could I get some food for him. His eyes open wide with fury. *It's only a dog, man! Now get in there!* He pushes me ahead of him and tells me to sit on a green silk cushion before a low coffee table, while he sits on the other side, propped up on three cushions, so he can be my height. On the coffee table between us is the large paperback he retrieved from his room. He picks it up with reverence, as if it was a sacred text. He kisses it and hands it to me. *In a moment, you'll read it to me*, he says and pulls out a plastic bag from a pocket in his shorts. He opens it and I smell the unmistakable odour of marijuana. *I prefer a bong, but these Taliban guys think it's a sign of Western decadence.* I watch him expertly roll a huge joint and light it with a cigarette lighter. He takes a huge puff, holds the smoke in his throat for a long time and then slowly exhales. *This is pure weed, no tobacco to ruin the high. Prime stuff. I mean Afghan stuff is the best in the world.* He hands me the joint. My shake of the head makes him laugh. *Gee, you're not like the Yanks – they love weed.*

As he takes a few more tokes he relaxes visibly. The dope is so strong, I'm getting a second-hand high; I'm feeling light-headed and, despite my desperate situation, I'm feeling relaxed. Not only that but I'm sorely tempted by it. It amuses me to think he doesn't know I was a stoner. Holy hell, was I ever. After Casey left Emerald Creek I spent most of my free time with stoners and slackers (not that there was much difference). We'd sit on the old machinery, pull bongs and drink cask wine. In winter I liked to get high and walk up the snow-covered hill and stare at the burning soil, the steam pouring out of the dead earth. You'd swear the steam heat was killing shrubs and trees right in front of you. The dope was all I would think about. I'd start with a few bongs before going to school, then have joints during morning and afternoon breaks and, of course, lunchtime. Then back home I'd sit on the creek bank watching the water, stoned out of my mind, listening to spacey dubstep stuff like *Burial* or dark drone metal like *SunnO)))* on my headphones until the early hours of the morning, becoming more and more obsessed by it. I seemed to spend all my waking hours stoned. I only realised I had a problem with it when one of the boys I mixed with, a guy who smoked even more weed than I did, if that was possible, began to hear voices and become so paranoid that he threatened to kill his family. Even so, it was truly hard to quit and I'd promise myself I'd only smoke one joint and no more – but I could never stop at one. And now I find myself in the middle of Afghanistan sitting opposite a stoner midget.

After a few more puffs of the joint he taps the book,

signalling me to start reading. It's a comic book called *Bloom County* and has a cartoon on the cover of a penguin with a gigantic nose. *Opus*, says Ghulam as if answering my question. *That's his name.* The pages are fragile, tissue-thin, as if the book has been read every day for years. He gets me to speak the dialogue in the different voices of the characters, even though he knows it word for word because he softly echoes everything I say. He giggles a lot, as if hearing it for the first time. It's difficult to make sense of the characters; there's a hard-drinking sleazebag bachelor always wearing sunglasses and making crude passes at women, a verbose rabbit, a black bespectacled kid with a genius IQ, a smart-talking cockroach, two young boys, a wheelchair-bound ex-Vietnam War veteran, Opus, the main character, and a scrawny, scruffy Bill the Cat with pinned eyes, who takes drugs and drinks too much. It's when I come to the cat that I understand Ghulum's strange strangling noises. Bill the Cat doesn't talk, but in constantly trying to bring up hairballs, cries out *Ack! Ack!* Whenever I imitate Bill the Cat's cough, I have to repeat it until I get the tone right. Each time Ghulum shakes his head in admiration, as if the sounds were the cleverest things he has ever heard.

I finish reading the comic book and he takes it from me, holding it tenderly against his tiny chest. *Captain*

Duncan gave it to me, before he finished his tour. He used to read it out to me. He did all the voices, really well, not like you. His Ack!Ack! . . . well, man, I'd fall on the floor laughing. That Bill the Cat is a crazy dude. No?

Yes, I say, having been unable to make sense of the comic strip. Ghulum places it on the table and gazes adoringly at it as if it's the most precious relic in the whole world.

I have to stop from giggling as I look at him perched on the cushions, smoking a joint, wearing ridiculous clothes, the revolver at his side. The strong smoke is making my head spin. I glimpse a shadow at the doorway and see Prince peering in, not daring to enter. I become aware of a soft, grating noise and realise that Ghulum is grinding his teeth again. He glances at me, seemingly irritated, but whether it's with me, Prince, or someone else, I have no idea. He rocks slightly as if trying to relax. Beads of sweat break out on his forehead and he gives me such an evil stare that he looks like a demon. I recognise the symptoms – he's such a heavy dope smoker that he's becoming paranoid. I smile, trying to find a way of making me less threatening. *I really like* Bloom County. *When I get back to Australia I'll track down other issues.*

Ghulum does a comic double-take. *I don't think you'll ever see Australia again.*

With that he grabs his gun and gets to his feet. *Carry that!* he orders, pushing the book across at me. *And be careful with it, man.* He directs me outside. *Get that damn dog away from me*, he squeals as Prince comes to greet me, his stump of a tail wiggling with happiness. I wave him away, not wanting him to annoy a tense Ghulum as we cross to the opposite side of the compound. *You see, man, I gotta do this, 'cos I really don't trust you.* He steps aside from a doorway and waves me in. The door squeaks open, the bottom rubbing against the floor. I almost reel with the smell. The stench is unbelievable; it's as if I'm about to enter a filthy lavatory stinking of human shit, piss and sick.

Go in, man. This is gonna be your new home. He stands a few metres from me, pointing the revolver at me. He's jittery and biting his lips. I hear a moaning, like a sick animal, coming from inside the room. Ghulum grins, *Hey, dude, I hope you get on with them.*

I step inside the dark, stinking room and see a figure in the shadows. A man squeals like a rabbit caught in a steel trap. Then something stirs in the corner and there's a scurrying sound on floorboards. I turn on hearing the soft footsteps of Ghulum come up behind me. *Meet the folks*, he says, in his high-pitched voice.

He opens the door further so that sunlight creeps in. I'm trying not to gag. Once my eyes become used to the dim light, I make out a naked man in the far corner and another one, opposite him, wearing only black shorts. The men are filthy; their hair is matted and their skin stained with shit and urine. One huddles into the corner as if trying to merge into the stone wall. The other one is grinning wildly, displaying his broken, rotting teeth. He suddenly throws himself at me. I flinch, and at the same time he seems to leap backwards. I see the cause; both arms and a leg are tied with ropes which are attached to a thick metal ring, the size of a basketball hoop, hammered into the wall. The two men seem more like beasts than humans.

They've gone bananas, says Ghulum answering my thoughts. The man cringing in the corner begins to hiss at me like a snake. The effort is so violent that he's soon foaming at the mouth. *This is what your boys did to them. Me, I'd put them out of their misery, but they're our commander's cousins. He has this wacko idea that they've got the devil inside them and says they'll be cured when you guys leave the country. Me? I think they're nuts forever.*

He tells me that both men had been Taliban commanders but had gone mad, one slowly over time, the other when he returned home to his village to find that his wife and five children had been killed by a bomb and buried only a few hours before his arrival. *You guys,* says Ghulum, tugging at my sleeve to get my attention, *have sent the whole country crazy. But you know, you lost! We've seen off the British, the Russians and now you Aussies and Americans. Losers!*

While he's berating me, the man in the corner shivers as if having a fit. I can't believe the misery they live in, having to be tied up twenty-four hours a day, living and sleeping in their own muck. The one that tried to rush me twists his head and stares at me, like a waterbird tilting its head to avoid the reflected sunlight on the water so as to see under the surface. His face softens and he bows towards me as if before an emperor. *Excuse me, excuse me,* he says in a thick accent.

The loon knows some English, so whattaya know, first time I've heard it from him. Hey, Corporal, Ghulum says loudly as I stare at the naked madman continuing to bow and repeat, like a mantra, *Excuse me, Excuse me.* Ghulum gets my attention by punching me in the side. *You three will have a lot to talk about, Corporal, and you can tell them why you guys have driven them bonkers. Ack! Ack! I need another joint.* He pauses as if he's thinking of lighting up one immediately, then he turns and points to a third metal ring, with a rope tied to it. *Used to be three, but the dickhead chewed through his ropes, escaped, got a knife from the kitchen and tried to kill the commander's wife . . . and then there were two. But now it'll be three again. Let's hope the guys don't take their time getting back, or else by the time they find you, man, you'll be as loony as these dipsticks.*

I want to run. This place stinks of sickness. These men are crazy. The stench makes me want to throw up. If there's a hell, then this is it. A shadow flicks past the doorway. We both spin around. It's only Prince. He walks in carefully and suspiciously, as if he too is appalled by the stink. *Ack! Ack!* Ghulum screams at him, but Prince can't hear and pauses a couple of metres from the both of us, his forehead crinkled in a deep frown. *Tell that damn dog to go!*

He's deaf.

Good, then he won't hear himself die. With that Ghulum points the gun at Prince and, before I can react, he fires. There's the sound of a shot, followed immediately by a sharp metallic ping. Prince doesn't react but there's a gentle sigh from Ghulum. He stares at his own blood staining the image of the cute child on his chest and then looks at me, a bewildered expression on his face, before he pitches forward and, with a soft thud, his body hits the floorboards. One of the madmen starts to cry out to Allah. I'm stunned and for a few moments I can't move. Then I work out what happened. The bullet missed Prince, hit one of the metal rings and ricocheted into the midget.

The chained men go quiet. I bend down and turn over the body. It's so light, almost weightless. Ghulum has the contented expression of a sleeping child. Prince sniffs the corpse, as if trying to find an explanation for this strange event. The comic book lies on the floor near the body. It's probably the only possession Ghulum had; one that reminded him of another time and better place. The thing that strikes me again is how chance determined that he should die, and Prince live.

Staring down at the body I hear a noise and see one of the men slapping his face, crying out words I don't understand. I'm suddenly aware that I've got no time to waste. We have to leave as soon as possible. The Taliban could be on their way back right now. I don't want to hang around because they'll think I killed Ghulum. I need to pick up my guns from the opium-processing room, grab some food from the kitchen and make tracks.

I'm on my way out of the room when I hear, *Excuse me, Excuse me.* I look back at both men. I have never seen such human wretchedness. The one in the corner seems to be abusing me in Pashto, while the other keeps bowing at me. I can't leave without freeing them and I cut their ropes. The one in the corner is the first to realise he is free and, like an animal, crawls past me to the outside, where he kneels and stares at the sky, loudly thanking Allah. The other gradually understands he is free too. He takes a few steps towards me, clasps my hand and shakes it fiercely as if he is using my arm as a pump, endlessly repeating, *Excuse me, Excuse me.*

There's nothing more I can do for them, and Prince and I leave the stinking hole and run to the processing room to get my rifle and revolver. The opium room's sickly-sweet smell is a relief after the hellhole. Picking up my rifle and revolver, I rush out into the courtyard and head for the kitchen. One of the madmen, naked and covered in grime, is pushing the garden wheelbarrow towards the other man, who is lying in the dirt on his back, staring at the sky. I hear a shrill noise and look up. A jet is flying low, directly at the compound. It passes overhead, the underside of the plane white like a shark's. Two rockets emerge from puffs of smoke under its wings. I throw myself onto the ground as the rockets explode on the far side of the compound with deep, thudding booms. The ground wobbles. A row of fireballs and a column of thick black smoke rise high in the air. The kitchen and reception area I had been making for only seconds ago is obliterated before my eyes. They're now just burning ruins.

There's a whine in the sky and I see another plane, coming closer and lower at a breathtaking speed. Prince is staring at the destruction, trying to make sense of it. I snatch him by the collar and we run to the front gates. We pass one of the madmen trying to lift the other one into the wheelbarrow. I stop, and with one heave throw the second man into the barrow. Then before I can move, a plane is right above us and two rockets overshoot the compound and detonate in a blast that stuns me. I look to the south and see the tiny outline of another jet coming towards us.

Prince and I run out of the compound. I turn back on hearing more explosions and see that most of the buildings are on fire. The wheelbarrow emerges from the black clouds of smoke, with one of the madmen sitting inside it, while the other, laughing wildly, pushes it through the gates.

That seems to be the last of the planes. We're safe for now. Gazing at the destroyed buildings the thought occurs to me – the Taliban must have found out about the bombing raid and had fled. I hear the cry of *Excuse me! Excuse me!* The madman is pushing the barrow towards me but my attention is taken by a noise behind me and I spin around. A jet is coming in, this time from the east. Prince and I have nowhere to hide. I see two rockets coming directly towards us and instinctively I grab Prince in a bear hug and fall to earth with him, closing my eyes and readying myself. The ground bounces. The deep and powerful roar makes my ears ring and my insides shudder like jelly. Dust and pebbles rain down on me. I feel dazed and weak but force myself to sit up. The madman, now covered in a grey powder, is still pushing his wheelbarrow towards me, completely unconcerned that he just missed being obliterated. Both men are laughing as if life has become just a big joke to them.

In a couple of hours it'll be dark. I feel groggy but know we must head west to the valley for water and food. *Come on, Prince*, I say, thinking he's beside me. But he isn't. He's vanished. I stagger to my feet and look around. There's a chill feeling in the pit of my stomach. I must have let go of him when the bomb hit. All I can hear is the constant cry of *Excuse me, Excuse me!*

In the distance I see what looks like a faint black dot heading over a distant crest. The exploding earth, smoke and chaos must have spooked Prince into fleeing. There is nothing else to do but go after him.

The madmen pause a few metres from me. They're covered in a ghostly, white-greyish dust. I point to the distant hills. *My dog, I have to get my dog.* They giggle as if amused by my plight. I start off at a slow jog. I know I have to pace myself in the heat but the fear of losing him drives me on. As I set out, the two men, one in the wheelbarrow, the other pushing it, head off into the desert, whistling happily.

9

Before long I slow down to a walk. I stop often to see any signs of Prince, but it's as if he's been swallowed up by the earth. The only thing I can do is aim for the valley. I'm counting on the fact that he will smell the water and is making for the river too. I feel awfully weary, and my insides are still quivering from the explosions, but I keep moving.

A few days ago I would have been annoyed that Prince had run off but now I can understand why he did. I know I'm in a war, he doesn't. The sniffing out of roadside mines is a game to him. After he's found one, the only reward he wants is to play with his square ball. This is a war between humans and he has been caught up in it through no wish of his own. Now he's deaf, he's been shot, he's struggled through unbearable heat, and he's had the ground blow up around him. On top of that he's lost Casey and he's ended up with me. No wonder he took off.

I can't let him or Casey down. Prince is my comrade now and my friend, so I'm not going to leave him behind. The very thought that he may die or I won't be able to find him eats away at me.

I travel across ridges and dips, swells and bluffs. Night's coming when I crest a flat-topped mound, and my heart soars when I see the dark ribbon of the stream winding its way along the valley floor. A couple of kilometres to the right are the lights of a hamlet. That means there are fields nearby and therefore fruit and vegetables. I sip the last of my warm water and walk carefully down the steep hill, in a zigzagging pattern. My hope is that Prince is already there, having found the water.

When I reach the valley I walk alongside the stream, searching for him. The waning moon isn't as bright as it's been the past few days so it's harder to see. A shadow seems to move, as if it's Prince. My heart prickles with hope but it's not him. I continue for several hours moving back and forth across the stream, eating pomegranates, the only ripe food available.

My exhaustion finally gets the better of me and I flop down beside the stream, remove my boots and soak my aching, blistered feet in the water, wondering what to do next. Where is he? Has he already found the stream and having rested is now making for . . . making for where? What would have been on his mind after he stopped running and found himself alone? Would he have doubled back to search for me, or is he still spooked and wandering aimlessly? There are those other terrible thoughts: what if he's been shot? Or has died in the heat?

The possibilities are endless and I realise I that I will have to search for him during the day, as it will be easy to miss him at night. I have to believe that he's alive. My aim will be to follow the river southwards in the hope that he'll stay close to water, especially during the long, hot days.

I've never felt so alone. I try to stop myself from feeling that I will not find Prince or make it back. I'm so tired and afraid that I have little mental strength left. I sit in the stream to cool down, as my mother used to do, not caring that my boots and clothes are soaking. The water soothes me and I wash my face clean of self-pity. I can't allow these things to get the better of me. I find a hollow space in an embankment along the river and curl up inside it to sleep.

I wake on hearing a cry of pain above me and realise it's one bird calling to another. Because of the way I've slept, my shoulder throbs painfully, and I go through a series of exercises to relieve the soreness. I don't want to take another morphine tablet, as I only have the one left. Getting ready I'm aware of an empty feeling in my stomach. I've had no food except for the pomegranates. If Prince is alive then he too must be hungry, unless he has caught some animal.

I keep on along the river bank and rest in any shade I find on the way. I take a break under a tree and I'm about to get up and continue when I hear distant shouts and what sounds like a shot. I fall onto my stomach and peer over the long grass. A group of boys is playing cricket in the baking heat. They have three sticks for stumps and a bat carved out of a hunk of wood. The ball seems to be made of wood too, because it hits the bat with a loud crack.

As I watch, I forget where I am. It's like a game of cricket anywhere. There's the laughter, the loud appeals for a catch, the protests of the batsmen given out. There's much good-natured teasing and of course there's the badly co-ordinated boy whose throw goes the wrong way, the one who is better at the game than anyone else, two nerdy boys meandering around the field chatting to each other paying no attention to what is happening, the fast bowler with his long run-up and the spinner tossing up slow full tosses that are whacked out of the field with the loud crack of a gun being fired.

It seems such a long time ago that I was just a normal kid like them playing cricket. It makes me feel ancient, though I'm not even nineteen yet. My birthday is in two days' time. Casey and I were given leave to go into Kabul to celebrate it when we returned. He was still kidding me about it the night before we went, *I never thought a gronk like you would make nineteen*. Perhaps he was right, perhaps I won't make my birthday.

Just after noon the boys pack up and head back to their village for lunch. Keeping a careful eye out, I take a wide detour around the village and make my way along the river, which is slowing to a trickle. A couple of hours later I spot a small village. It has a white domed mosque and one street with ramshackle buildings either side of it. I'm debating with myself how much distance I want to keep between me and it when I realise that there don't seem to be any people. There's a chance that Prince is in there looking for food.

The aroma of spices and animal and human muck fills my nostrils as I walk towards the house. I pause outside a mud wall and make sure the village is empty. It seems safe, so I set out down the only street. The buildings are either boarded up or their metal window shutters are half closed or warped. Mud stalls are collapsing. How did this end up a ghost town of collapsed houses and bombed-out shops? Clumps of grass are sprouting around the shops, which still smell of exotic spices. It must have been an important market, bustling and noisy, in contrast to its unnerving silence now. Judging by the desolation it's been abandoned for a year or more.

I look everywhere but I can't find Prince or any evidence of him. The heat is unbearable and I seek out the shade of a mud-brick house where the front door is barely clinging from its hinges. As I brush by the door, it breaks free and falls onto the ground. I step over it and walk inside to be greeted by an upturned table, several smashed chairs and broken glass. Despite the mess, it's cooler than outside. I sit down on the hard dirt floor and as I drink some water I hear a sound, like someone moving. My heart stops, I pick up my rifle and glance over my shoulder in the direction the noise has come from. There's another room without a door. I listen but hear nothing. Maybe I've imagined it or else it might have been a rat. I'm about to put down my rifle, when I hear something like a groan or grunt.

Moving as quietly as I can, I step to the side of the doorway. Adrenalin surges through me, my hands are damp with fear. I listen closely; nothing is stirring or moving. I look around the door frame into the window-less room. It's dark except for a tiny flickering light in the corner where a thin Afghan, wearing brown baggy trousers, a white T-shirt and brown turban sits before a candle. His gaze is focused on something in his hands and he doesn't seem aware I'm watching him. He places a thin metal pipe in his mouth and puts a strip of foil onto the candle flame. On the foil is a brown pool of resin. He strikes a match and places it under the foil and tilts it so that the resin slides downwards as he inhales. His eyes close and he smiles blissfully to himself: he begins to rock slightly. Then his body jolts as if hit by an electric charge and he spins around on his backside, staring goggle-eyed at me. His surprise becomes a frown. The longer he looks at me the more puzzled he becomes until he shakes his head, as if freeing himself of a bad vision. He wearily waves me away as one would a phantom. When I don't move, he lifts up his right hand at me and, pretending it's a gun, points two fingers at me, making a soft shooting noise – then, apparently believing he has killed the enemy soldier standing in the doorway, he turns his attention back to the opium and carefully dabs more on to the foil. He's not so much a human being as a living skeleton, all alone with only his addiction for company. It's certain he isn't long for this world. Before he can put the foil on the candle flame again, he sighs with satisfaction, closes his eyes, and slowly falls backwards until he lies on the floor, drifting off into his own dream world.

Even though the fellow poses no threat to me, I'm worried that there may be other Afghans around, so

I set off again, trudging through the heat, looking for Prince. What I cannot shake from my mind are images of Ghulum and now this addict in the empty room. I've never seen two such broken and lonely men. The thought crosses my mind that if I were Afghan and my country had been at war so long, would I have ended up like them?

Hours later I come upon another deserted hamlet. The irrigation channels leading to it are dry and the fields are overgrown with weeds. I make sure there are no locals around and I'm about to walk down the main street when I see a movement near a crumbling mosque. I catch my breath. It's a dog. I start running towards it but as I get closer I notice that it's not black and is larger and scruffier than Prince. It's joined by two other dogs. I stop in my tracks. These are not dogs but wolves, scrounging around the compound for food.

I've seen Afghan wolves before, silently casing a village or setting on a pack of wild goats. Because of drought in this part of the country the locals have had to sell or eat their flocks to survive. This has changed the balance of nature. Before the long dry the wolves would have picked off the odd sheep, but now that there are few sheep or goats left the wolves have been moving in on the only available food source: people.

Children have been snatched and killed at night and now the wolves are becoming so bold there are reports they are attacking people during the day.

On hearing me approach the three wolves take a few steps forward and stare directly at me. I know that if I run they'll see me as prey. I stand as still as I can and hope that there is no wind to carry my scent. For some minutes we stare at each other until the wolves, perhaps unable to decide whether I am prey or not, slowly head back into the hills.

It's evening when I find refuge in a clump of oaks on the side of the stream opposite orchards and poppy fields. I'm so tired and hungry and full of disappointment that I haven't found Prince or any signs of him that all I can do is slump in the undergrowth beneath a tree. My face is burning with the heat and I can feel moisture in my socks where the blisters, on the soles of my feet, have burst. It's all I can do to stop from falling into despair and giving up my search for Prince and even the aim of making it home. How will I find the strength to continue?

In the morning I wake up on hearing excited cries. There are a dozen or so children running across a paddock, launching kites into the air. The kites are blue, green and red and they dip and rise in the air currents. The boys and girls squeal with delight and make gunfire noises, pretending to be planes attacking each other. Two kites become caught up and fall to the ground just on the edge of the oak grove. I'm close enough to see that the two boys are wearing blue and red eyeliner. They untangle their kites and launch them again. I watch them rise into the blue sky. They look beautiful.

The trouble is that I'm trapped. The marijuana and poppy plantations on the other side of the river come right down to the water's edge and if I break cover from my hiding place I'll be easily seen. I'll have to wait for everyone to return to the village.

Teenage girls and old men with long white beards slowly move through the sea of poppies, scoring the green pods with razor blades so that the brown resin rises to the surface like sticky, rubbery pus. When I arrived in Afghanistan I was amazed at how many poppy fields there were. But for many Afghans the crop is the only way of earning money. One opium farmer laughed when he told me he didn't mind war because blood was a good fertiliser. I had no idea whether he was having me on or not, but then Afghans are so used to war that normal values don't count. The coalition armies had to allow the cultivation to continue if they didn't want to turn the locals against them.

All I can do over the next few hours is observe village life, in a way I haven't before. It seems so normal. Every time I've come upon a farmer or entered a village the adults and children have been on their guard. It's always tense, because you have no idea if they are the Taliban or just ordinary people who might have a personal grudge against us foreigners.

I see them go about their business as if there is no war. The workers harvest throughout the stifling day. A couple of motorbikes roar out of the village and go north. Girls with buckets on their heads collect water from a well on the outskirts of the village. It amazes me how the women are able to move around in their burqas. Most are covered head to toe, with a crocheted grille across the eyes which gives them such limited side vision that they are always bumping into things, and in a city like Kabul they're run over by cars because they can't see them coming.

I'm daydreaming when there's the sound of women not far from me and the splash of water. I crawl back further into the long grass. There's giggling and more splashing. Three women, having removed their head-gear, are standing in the shallows of the river and cooling their flushed faces with water. I've never seen Afghan women smiling and laughing. Usually they're either wrapped inside a burqa or glaring at you, full of suspicion and hate. These three are about sixteen or seventeen. One has long black hair down to her shoulders. She reminds me of my ex-girlfriend; the same hair, the same laugh that makes her face light up.

Poor Lucia. She said that what made her go for me was that I made her laugh, unlike her previous boyfriend who was always too serious. It wasn't long, though, before she began to complain about my dope-smoking and the fact that even in my final year of high school, I had no idea what I wanted to do with my life. *You've got to get out of Burning Mountain*, she'd say, *there's no future here*. She was going to leave, and why didn't I? But the life of a slacker suited me.

It all came to an end one night when we were in Wrightsville after seeing a movie. I had smoked a joint in the toilets before we set off back to Emerald Creek. Lucia was annoyed with me but there was no other car for her to go home in except for my bomb. I was so stoned that I didn't realise just how angry she was with me. In fact, her criticisms made me laugh, which infuriated her even more. Near a turnoff I took the corner too sharply and the car slid across the muddy road and hit a tree. There was the sound of crunching metal and the windscreen shattering. Far from being shocked, I felt detached, as if I was watching a movie about the crash. I looked across at Lucia, who had shards of sparkling glass in her black hair and in her lap, but seemed unhurt. Once I realised I was fine too,

I started to laugh, thinking it was the funniest thing, until I became aware of a strange noise next to me – Lucia was weeping.

You're just a boy! You don't care about anyone but yourself! she cried, and when I went to stroke her arm she pushed me away and, jumping out of the car, called me an idiot, a gronk. Then she walked off into the night.

And I was a gronk, an idiot, a total jerk. It wasn't a surprise when she broke up with me. I knew that the way I lived and behaved was the cause, but I couldn't give up dope – and the wonderful thing about weed is that the more you smoke, the more it eases the pain of someone leaving you. She didn't wait until the end of the year to escape Emerald Creek and become a nanny in Scotland. I barely passed Year 12 and I lazed around, smoking bongs, watching DVDs of *Family Guy* and perfecting my Stewie voice. Then one evening, as I was drinking cask wine on top of the burning mountain, stoned out of my gourd, I found myself staring at the steam escaping from cracks in the earth and I was struck by just how alien the countryside looked: how scarred, how like Hell. At that moment I knew my future was like the wasteland around me, empty of promise.

Even so, it was difficult to give up weed, until one night I heard footsteps in the corridor. They didn't sound like Dad's. I put down my bong and looked out my bedroom door. I saw a figure with its back to me. It turned around. It was Mum, wearing the red slippers. She seemed as if she was going to say something but instead walked slowly on into the darkness and vanished. The sight spooked me. Either the ghost was real or else my pot-smoking was messing with my mind. Whatever it was, I took it as a warning that I needed to get my life back together.

Only by leaving Burning Mountain would I have a future. I left for Sydney, went cold turkey and worked as a shelf-stacker and labourer. Dad had wanted me to study engineering but my science marks were poor, and besides, I didn't want to follow in his footsteps because I knew I wouldn't be as good an engineer as he was. Sydney didn't solve my problems and I was afraid I would return to my messy ways when one day I saw a soldier in uniform and his wife leaving a supermarket. There was something about his maturity, his sureness, that appealed to me. I knew I needed a purpose in my life or else I'd end up a total loser. Typically it was Dad's opposition to me joining up that made me do so. *You'll never make it. You don't have what it takes, son,* he told me and during the first few months he was right. I hated obeying orders. Most of them seemed so trivial and pointless that I felt like leaving every day until the captain called me into his office and dressed me down for my attitude. *I'll show you and Dad*, I thought to myself, and I stuck it out in order to stick it up them. Well, I've certainly shown them: here I am on the run, hiding in the grass trying not to be killed . . . that's really sticking it to them.

The woman who looks like Lucia becomes serious, as do her friends. They step out of the water, the bottom of their burqas dark with water. They slip their hoods back on as if putting on a mask and walk into the village.

Not long afterwards, two black four-wheel-drive vehicles appear, escorted by motorbikes, horns blaring as they drive into the village. The boys grab their kites and hurry after the cars, excited and yelling at the top of their voices. Three jingle trucks arrive, painted psychedelic colours, and decorated with tassels and flags and ornamental chains, chimes and bells, as if they are part of a circus rather than work vehicles. Obviously there are no dogs in the village or else they would have been barking.

With the arrival of the trucks, the poppy workers race each other back home. The orchards and fields are suddenly empty of people. It's an eerie feeling. Why has everyone dropped tools and headed back to the village? I move as carefully as I can through a marijuana crop to the ragged rows of wild grapevines. I stop when I hear the sounds of shots. Six men are standing in the main street shooting at the sky. Behind them women in blue or white burqas scurry across the dusty street. Music and singing break out, and I realise that the people are celebrating a wedding.

The guests will be so preoccupied that it should be easy for me to go around the village and return to following the river a few kilometres downstream. I can only hope that Prince is still in the valley, heading south like me. As I make my detour, I see children in the village swapping sweets, playing tag and putting eyeliner on each other. Two of them, one missing a leg and another with a wooden peg, cling to each other and cry with happiness as they dance in a circle while others clap and sing.

Another movement catches my eye. Five men, all in Taliban black, are walking a black dog across the street with a rope around its neck. I stop in my tracks, I can't believe it. But there's no mistaking him; it's Prince. Prince is alive!

The men pause and one of them arranges the group to be photographed on his mobile phone. They're proud and smiling, as if they have captured a high-ranking soldier. My flesh tingles with happiness on seeing Prince, but just how he has ended up with the enemy is a mystery. Maybe they caught him after tempting him with food.

After taking more pictures, the Taliban march Prince behind a mud wall. Panic strikes me; are they going to kill him? I listen carefully, praying not to hear a shot. I watch for him to appear again but all I see are excited children running back and forth playing games. How can I get him back? To rescue him will be impossible during the celebrations, with so many Taliban at the wedding. I'll have to wait for an opportunity to find him and escape without being seen. All I know is that I'm going to attempt it. I'm resolved; I either get back to base with Prince, or not at all.

What concerns me is what they intend to do with him. Afghans loathe dogs. One of the worst things you can call someone is a dog. The locals breed them for fights. I've seen plenty of those poor mutts, chained up and maddened by their fights, their bodies scarred and torn, their owners oblivious to the dogs' hunger and pain. Casey said that far from being afraid Prince would calmly stare at them, as if he knew that their fury was a sign of madness, not hatred.

The wedding continues into the early evening when the two four-wheel-drive cars and the noisy jingle trucks, packed with guests, head back the way they came. After the final call to prayers from the mosque, lights come on in the houses. Over the next couple of hours I watch as each light goes off. It's frustrating. Usually villages don't keep their lights on for long but it seems as if the wedding celebrations are continuing. Near midnight the last light is switched off and the village is finally quiet. The moon is dropping below the snow-covered mountains and I'll have little light to see by. It will make it easier for me to hide in the darkness but it'll be harder for me to find Prince.

As I move towards the houses and shacks, I tread as softly as possible on the hard earth and pebbles. In the darkness I can make out the shapes of the buildings and the narrow alleyways between them. I am concentrating so hard on not making a noise that I can hear the blood surging through my head. I have no idea how many Taliban are in the village, but if they see me, I'm dead.

If Prince is still in the village then he'll be outside and tied up, because Islam forbids dogs inside a home. I slowly circle each house in turn, finding nothing. As I'm crossing a dirt courtyard at the rear of a house a light comes on inside and, without warning, the back door swings open. I've just got time to drop behind a large wooden crate. A man wearing a turban emerges from the house and trots towards the box. I pull out my revolver, ready to shoot. I hold my breath. I won't fire unless it's absolutely necessary because if I do there's little chance of me being able to get out of here alive.

He stops on the other side of the crate and hums a tuneless song. As he does so I hear the tinkle of water against the wood; then after a satisfied grunt, the man returns inside and the light goes off. I'm filled with a mixture of relief but also want to laugh – if only the fellow realised that I was on the other side of the box listening to him pissing.

The village looked small from a distance but it has about forty dwellings. As I check out each house I catch the familiar smells of sweets, spices and human waste. It grows cold, and once the moon completely disappears only the faint glow reflected into the sky above the mountain range helps me see. A couple of times I trip over objects lying in the darkness or slip on shale. Each time I freeze, expecting that I've been heard, but no lights come on. I squeeze down a narrow path running alongside the mosque to a clump of ten or so mud houses. I go from one to the next trying to find Prince in the shadows. I creep around the back of a house and can make out the outline of a truck on blocks in the yard, two of its wheels missing. I'm about to continue my search next door when I see a lump, like a bag. I creep closer and stop – my heart jumps, there's no mistaking it, it's a dog and the dog is Prince, balled up to keep out the cold. The fear he may be dead almost paralyses me, then I see the faint rise and fall of his body as he sleeps. A rope is around his neck and tied to the front bumper bar of the rusting truck. His deafness is probably the reason why he hasn't heard me. I have to wake him and at the same time stop him from barking in surprise.

I crawl on my hands and knees to him. He's snoring softly. I touch his muzzle, softly running my fingers over his whiskers so that he'll wake slowly. His eyes spring open and he jumps up in shock, not recognising me. He goes to bark but I clasp both hands over his muzzle. His body stiffens. I hold my hands tightly on his muzzle until I'm sure he recognises me. When he does I let go. Then, as if he feels he has done something bad, he crawls on his belly to me and gently licks my hand. I almost break down and weep. Why would he think he had done wrong? I hug him tightly as I have no one before, only stopping when he whimpers and I realise his wound is still painful. I stroke him, whispering his name in his ear even though I know he can't hear me. I untie the rope. Once free he does his strange little prancing dance around me, his stump of a tail wiggling furiously. I signal for him to stop because when he's truly excited he makes a high-pitched gurgling sound as if he was trying to sing. I whisper for him to be quiet and, although he's deaf, he knows to be silent.

I take a closer look at him. He seems healthy, though it's hard to see in the dark. I look around to make sure no one has heard or seen us and, grabbing him by the collar, make my way back around the mosque and out of the village, not looking back.

10

I only realise I have been holding my breath when a couple of hundred metres outside the village I fall to my knees to suck in deep gulps of air. Prince walks around me, concerned. *It's all right, mate*, I say when I'm breathing normally, *we're on our way home*.

We set off at a clip, we'll have to put a great distance between the Taliban and us before they discover that Prince has gone. If we continue back to base along the valley, chances are we will be spotted more easily than if we follow the contours of the hills to the west. It's a longer route but it might be safer.

We find ourselves on walking tracks. As they rise higher the paths narrow, hugging the bluffs and cliffs and leaving immense drops on the side. A false step means death. Each switchback is steeper than the last.

As morning comes, I find that we're walking on a goat trail about half a metre wide. A cliff face towers over us on the left and on the right it's a sudden drop into the valley. The dizzying sight of the valley floor far below makes my heart hammer in my chest. Prince trots ahead of me with that beautiful prancing gait that makes it seem as if he's not touching the ground. Seeing Prince so strong and noble fills me with confidence.

The sunlight shines on the eastern slopes and when we reach the crest of one I make out a cluster of caves about a kilometre away. They seem an obvious place to shelter from the sun. I'm daydreaming about finally being able to rest when I hear a footfall in front of me. I stop, petrified. There is nowhere for me to run or hide. I point my rifle and hope for the best. Prince's body goes rigid and he advances in the stiff-legged stalk he adopts when going to attack. His lips move as if he's muttering to himself. Then I see that ahead of Prince is a feral goat and behind him several others.

The goats realise they can't go forward or run around us as there's no room to move on the track. I call Prince to stop, but of course he can't hear me. I'm scared that he'll attack the lead goat and in the fight tumble over the side. The goat lowers its head and charges at Prince, its enormous curved horns gleaming in the morning sun. There seems to be no way of avoiding a clash but Prince leaps hard to his left as if trying to merge into the side of the bluff. The goat hits Prince on his right flank, ricochets off him and, unable to find its footing to steady itself, disappears down into the gorge, its bleats echoing around the hills. Alarmed, the others try to flee the way they have come. Two more fall into the abyss but the others manage to turn in the tight space and gallop off down the path, with Prince on their tail.

He chases them around the corner of the hill until they're out of sight. I can hear their shrill panic as he gains on them. I can't run for fear of losing my footing and so I walk as quickly as I can. I round the corner and come upon level ground the size of a basketball court. Prince has a young goat by the neck and they're rolling in the dust. He's silent and focused on his task, the goat bleating in fear and pain, its legs flailing wildly, its huge eyes filled with terror. It's the first time I have seen Prince killing another animal. His jaws are clamped on the neck with a ferocious, vice-like grip. He's no longer a soldier-partner but a predator so desperate for food that he'll fight to the death for it.

As the two struggle, I can see that Prince is tiring. I can't shoot the goat, because it might give away our position. I pull out my knife and plunge the blade into the goat's stomach. It shudders, goes limp and is still. Prince is panting heavily, exhausted by the fight. The goat lies on its side, its blood seeping onto the dusty earth. I look at Prince, who sniffs at the animal as if checking it's not faking death. My stomach rumbles and I remember I haven't had meat for days. I lift up the goat and, carrying it in my arms, we make our way down the slope to a bluff rutted with caves. Prince must have hurt his leg again as his limp is worse, so it's slow progress.

We enter the first cave we come to, too weary to even think of any dangers we might find in there. The size of a living room, it has a dry dirt floor and smells of old animal dung. Prince's nose is very dry and I give him some water before I prepare our food. I've skinned rabbits and wallabies but never a goat. Perhaps because the animal is young it turns out to be a surprisingly easy thing to do. With one hefty yank I rip off its fur and lay the naked goat on the earth. As I look down at it I'm almost sorry for what I've done, but that feeling last only a short time; Prince needs to eat, and so do I.

There's no wood for a fire and I hack the goat into large pieces, giving Prince first choice. He chooses a shoulder and chomps down on it with the savagery of the truly hungry, aware of nothing else other than needing the fuel for his body. He tears at the flesh and crunches through the bone. I don't have his strong teeth and so I chop up the heart and, trying not to look at what I'm eating, I start to chew. Its soft rubbery texture and blood is repulsive, but I need the protein.

Long after I've finished, Prince continues to crunch and chomp, occasionally vomiting the meat back up and re-eating it. He stuffs himself until even he has had enough and, after licking his blood-soaked muzzle, lies down, resting his head in my lap and closing his eyes with a sigh of contentment. I run my hand over him, feeling for ticks or injuries. The wound is healing and he's free of vermin but it's only when my fingers run across his ribs that I grasp just how much weight he has lost. It seems that the Taliban didn't feed him, and the trek will have taken its toll as well. His fur has lost its sheen and something has bitten him on his top lip, which is slightly swollen. I almost cry on seeing how red and raw his pads are.

His soft snoring and the warmth of his body against mine comforts me. I can feel the beat of his heart against mine. I'm filled with a love for him so deep that it burns and prickles my body. He is a reminder that there are things greater than me. We're not like lovers, no, this is something more pure and simple. It's deeper because he doesn't expect anything in return, he just wants to be with me. He trusts me and I trust him because it's a matter of life and death. His nose is now moist. My life is in that nose. He's sniffed out mines and saved lives, and he'll do whatever it takes to save my life, and I'll do the same for him. He may live only in the present but so do I now. It's us two against the world.

I fall asleep sitting up against the wall, rifle at my side in case of predators. When I wake up late afternoon, the first thing I see is Prince gnawing a bone, trying to extract the marrow. I take out the map and study it. There are two ways of getting back. One is to continue directly south and cross over the mountains where it'll be highly unlikely we will run into the enemy; the other is to go east, pass along the valley and then cross the plains to a small village I visited a few weeks ago during an operation. The locals there seemed to support us, though, as I'd quickly learnt, their co-operation is always unpredictable, depending on whether the Taliban control the area.

The problems with the first alternative are that it will take three days, it will be bitterly cold and I doubt whether Prince and I can muster the stamina to deal with the snow and thin air. Making a break for the east means an easier trek of only two days but we will have to risk going through enemy territory. There's no real option for us – three days is too long.

Looking at Prince as he sits licking his chops with a dreamy expression of contentment, I know that we can't leave straight away. We both need to rest and recover the strength needed to make our final dash home. My shoulder wound is throbbing with soreness. Removing my shirt I groan on seeing the wound festering and squirming with maggots. How flies managed to get to it is beyond me. I swallow my last morphine tablet and scrape away the maggots and pus with my knife, then sprinkle Quick Clot on the wound and go outside to let the sun dry it.

As I gaze down into the valley, running like a thin green ribbon through the dead hills, I mentally map out the next section of our journey. If we leave tomorrow in the late afternoon we will be able to navigate down the steep slopes with the aim of arriving in the valley at night and then head south-east into the plains by late tomorrow morning.

I glance over my shoulder back into the cave and see that Prince is sleeping. I shake my head, still finding it difficult to believe the mess I'm in. The chopper explosion and Casey's dead eyes haunt me. *Not so cocky now, Mark, are you?* Tomorrow, or is it the next day, I will be nineteen. But I don't believe I'm an adult at all. Deep down I feel like one of those little boys lost in the Australian bush and waiting to be found.

When I told Dad I wanted to fight in Afghanistan he said nothing, but it was easy to see he was bitterly disappointed. War to him is totally senseless. His own father was in Vietnam as a lieutenant and was just a couple of years older than I am now. When he returned home, things seemed fine at first but then he took to alcohol and it unleashed what Dad said was *a fury at life*. Grandfather was always angry, raging about the state of the world or hitting out at his wife and children. He'd often come home from the pub with his face bloody and bruised, almost in triumph, as if he felt he deserved the beating. One night, as he made his drunken way back from the hotel, he drowned in Emerald Creek. Dad always suspected he'd done it on purpose, as if to escape his self-hatred.

Because of his father's behavior, Dad turned his back on anything that had to do with war or sports. He found solace in books and dreams of finding a way to re-open the mine. I avoided his study because it seemed I'd be intruding on his private world. Every wall had shelves overflowing with books. When I did go in there I was overwhelmed by it, as if the books were a part of him and his immense knowledge was suffocating me. I don't know if it was a reaction to this, but I didn't like reading. One huge wall of books was about engineering and mechanical matters, while another had long shelves of fiction and books on ancient Greece and Rome, some in Latin, which he had learned as a boy. Occasionally he'd show me his beautifully drawn plans and ideas, which were sketched out in lines, arrows and doodles; they'd intrigued me, but not the books.

A year or so after Mum died, Dad called me into his study. We sat in silence for a long time and I was beginning to wonder why he wanted me there when he stood up and plucked out a book bound in red leather from a whole set of identically coloured volumes. It was 20 000 *Leagues Under the Sea*. He sat down and started to read. This became our nightly ritual. He expected me to listen to him read until the wall clock chimed nine o'clock, when he'd slap the book shut. I'd say goodnight and leave the room knowing he'd be starting on a bottle of whisky, lost in his own thoughts and dreams.

Over the next two years he read me the novels that made up Jules Verne's *Extraordinary Journeys in the Known and Unknown Worlds*, including *Journey to the Centre of the Earth* and *Around the World in Eighty Days*. At first I was uncomfortable listening to him. There was no smalltalk; he'd launch directly into the section where he'd left off the previous night. After a while I began to understand that he was still grieving for my mother and this was the only way he could connect with me. To actually talk to me would be too hard for him – it would bring back too many memories. It was better that we had another sort of relationship, one based on a shared appreciation of Verne. As the months went on, I grew to like listening to my father's low, steady voice, which would occasionally become excited when Verne detailed the science behind a character's quest to discover new places, deep in the earth or in the sky, something that appealed to Dad's engineer's mind. I began to look forward to this strange intimacy, and with it came a fascination with the novels, especially 20 000 *Leagues Under the Sea*. The scenes where Captain Nemo and his Nautilus submarine stopped to explore exotic underwater worlds enchanted me. There were shells the size of cows, forests of seaweed, tropical coral with colours so bright they hurt the eye, technicolour fish, marine flowers shaped like giant blue trumpets, huge tree-like plants and oysters the size of plates. Yet these wonderlands contained dangers; I had nightmares about monstrous sea spiders so large they could swallow a man, and for weeks I couldn't get out of my mind the image of a drowning woman slowly sinking to the ocean floor, still clutching her dead baby, as ravenous sharks circled them. Every time I thought about it, all I could see was my mother's face on that of the drowning woman. Despite this, the sea seemed beautiful and mysterious, especially to a country boy like me who had never seen it.

I must have said something to Dad about never having been to a beach because one morning he told me to get into the car and we drove from the mountains down to the coast, where he parked between two sand dunes. It was a warm day, with a cloudless sky. We walked through the gap between the two dunes and stopped; before us, stretching to the horizon, was the ocean. I was in awe of its hugeness; all I had known were rivers and creeks. Beneath the flat surface I imagined Nemo's world of weird shapes, brilliant colours and a peculiar kingdom where it was sometimes impossible to tell the difference between animals and plants. My daydream was broken by Dad crying out something at the top of his voice. When he saw me looking at him, puzzled as to what he saying, he smiled and repeated what sounded like a foreign word. *It's 'Thalatta! Thalatta!'*, he said, excited, explaining that it was the cry of soldiers in the ancient Greek army that fought their way home through enemy territory, arriving at last at the shore and calling exultantly *The sea! The sea!* Dad shouted out the word again. *Come on, join me*, he said and we both cried out, *Thalatta! Thalatta!* The word seemed to release something in him, as if all the grief had been dammed up in him and now a breach – caused by the Greek word for sea – had been made. He shouted louder and I joined in. We continued until we both grew hoarse and we fell about laughing on the sand. Then I heard a strange groaning noise. Dad's body heaved as if he were vomiting up everything; every particle of grief, loss and confusion. Even though I was young, I knew that this purging would help him. I also knew there was nothing I could do, other than let him weep in private. I walked to the edge of the sea and imagined I was Captain Nemo in my submarine beneath the waves.

We stayed on the beach for over an hour before returning to Burning Mountain, but somehow the shouting had released Dad's pent-up grief. From then on he seemed to fall prey to dark moods less and less. He still read Verne to me but he began to make smalltalk and we would discuss the science, both bad and good, in the novels. *You know, Mark, it's only us*, he said one evening when I was about to go to bed. I looked at him, at his concerned face shining in the lamplight. I nodded, knowing that his parents were dead and that our few remaining relatives lived interstate, with none of them maintaining any ties to us. Dad was right, it was only us two.

One night I went ahead and spoiled it all when I came back home from drinking and smoking with my mates. I was heading off to my room when the study door opened and Dad poked his head out. *How about us finishing* Mistress Branican? he said. It was a novel about a French woman searching for her husband in Australia. I had been growing tired of Jules Verne and the novel had begun to bore me. *No, it's crap*. Dad frowned as if he couldn't believe what I said. *I'm no longer a kid!* I shouted and went on to my room where I lay on my bed, feeling guilty about what I'd said; but I wasn't going to apologise – and, being the dickhead I was, I never did.

He never brought up the subject again, but our worlds began to separate – it was as if Verne was the only connection we had and I had broken it. Although we were civil to each other, we kept to ourselves, with Dad retreating even more into his study and his private universe.

Before I left Burning Mountain for Afghanistan he followed me out to my car and when I was about to get in said quietly, *Plato believed that it's only the dead who have seen the end of war.*

That's damn typical, I thought, *his last words to me are a quote from a philosopher.* I went to hug him all the same, but he backed away. I thought, *Well, screw you!* and jumped in the car, driving away, not looking back. I was hurt but now I understand he didn't want to touch me. He thought his touch was a curse. By not hugging me he was hoping that I would come home unharmed. And now he has heard I am dead, he must think he is alone in the world.

My skin starts to burn and I return to the cave and see that Prince is still sleeping, his legs twitching as he dreams. He needs this rest as much as I do. A scorpion scuttles towards him and I get some satisfaction by crushing it under my boot.

I'm dozing when I wake up to the pleasant sensation of something warm and moist on my skin. I'm still not wearing my shirt and Prince is licking my shoulder wound. I'm amazed; he must know the wound has to heal. He doesn't look at me as he does it but concentrates on long licks. I can feel the saliva coating the cut. According to Casey, a dog's tongue carries healing antibodies. It can only help me. Prince steps away and stares at me, his mouth open, as if he's smiling, proud of his efforts. I scratch his throat. I want to praise him but I can't say anything because I would cry; his concern for me is extraordinary and I wonder if I am worthy of it. The only way I will be worthy of him is if I get him back safely.

Early in the evening we eat more of the goat. I pretend the uncooked meat is a Japanese dish and that it tastes better raw than cooked. Prince sits beside me, tearing at the stringy meat. I laugh at the sight of us chomping into the bloody hunks. I realise that I have become an animal too and we're both on the same level of the basic drive of life – eat to survive. Later, as the night turns cold, we curl up together for warmth. His fur feels soft against my skin. I notice our heartbeats are in sync. The sensation of it is soothing and I feel an incredible, reassuring sense of security being with him.

When we wake just before dawn I hear an annoying buzzing noise. The remains of the goat on the cave floor are fly-ridden. Prince doesn't seem interested in it any more, so I bury two legs in the dirt to dig up later and throw the rest outside.

Over the next three hours I sit in the shade of the cave entrance with Prince and watch the sun bake the soil. The landscape is as sterile as Mars. About four in the afternoon a shaft of sunlight inches its way into the cave. I get ready, check my M4 and pistol, dig up the two goat legs and stuff them in my backpack as emergency food for Prince. There are no rations or pain-killers left and only a small amount of Quick Clot. My wound has stopped throbbing, thanks to Prince. His leg has improved and the limp is less noticeable. The meat did wonders for him. His eyes sparkle with enthusiasm and he walks around, eager to be on the move. I motion him to wait. He sits in the shaft of sunlight as I examine the map again to make certain of our route. Where we will be travelling is a blank space except for four villages, all of which are unnamed, including the one we're aiming for.

I glance up from the map and see him staring outside, his fur shiny in the sunlight. He looks so noble, indeed like a prince. He turns to me, and at that moment the sun hits his eyes and I am astonished. It's as if the black film covering them has washed away to reveal their true colour – they are a deep blue. They are exactly as Casey described them. The eyes are beautiful and peaceful, as if they see beyond fear and worry. Casey was right, it's as if you can see into Prince's soul and he into yours. And as I gaze in wonder at him he blinks, and when his eyelids open the blackness, like a veil, covers his eyes again. *I can't make it without you. I know you understand that*, I say, hugging him.

11

It's still hot when we leave the cave, but we have to put up with the heat because it would be impossible to see where we are going. The route is downhill at first, later we'll have to follow the contours and hope to find animal or human tracks. Prince seems so much healthier and I feel better for the rest. He looks up at me, his head at a tilt as if he is silently asking me just how serious this next part of our journey will be. *Well, Prince, my boy,* I say, giving him a tap on the rump, *maybe a day and a half, maybe two.*

At first the going is easy because we've found goat trails, but then evening comes. The air is thin and cold and the physical effort is so taxing that I'm sweating and Prince's tongue is hanging out of his mouth. As the moon slips below the mountain ranges, it becomes increasingly difficult to see. Sometimes we lose the track and find ourselves on a cliff edge, with only a dark emptiness below. Once or twice I slip on loose stones and find myself sliding down a hill, only stopping when

I jam my boot heels into the hard earth. This spooks me and I have to sit for a while recovering my breath and try to slow my racing pulse. Our schedule is unravelling. We're taking much longer than I thought and at times I wonder if we're ever going to reach the valley.

It's when I find myself crawling on the earth trying to feel for a track that I spot a pale white patch in front of me. It's the back view of Prince – his rear hindquarters have a splash of white that stands out from his black fur. Casey had dyed it, as he had the white patch on his neck, but I suppose because Prince has been sitting most of the day in the cave, the black dye has worn away. I signal him to walk ahead of me. He knows what I want and he trots ahead, more certain of where the tracks are than I am in the dim light. I follow the small white patch as it sways slightly in the darkness like a lamp in a breeze. Because he's in front of me I can't tell him to slow down. He must sense I'm lagging behind, because sometimes he turns his head to see where I am and waits for me to catch up. It's as if he's leading a blind man, which in a way I am. Never have I been so dependent on another being.

When I think we must be close to the valley we instead find ourselves on a plateau that leads to more hills and switchbacks. We're following the contours of one slope when Prince pauses, staring intently at something in the

144

shadows. At first I think the ground is littered with large rocks, then as we come closer I see that there seems to be a rough purpose to their arrangement. Rocks and stones of unequal height, some up to a metre tall, seem to have been planted in the soil as if to make a stone garden. Prince sniffs the air like a wine connoisseur smelling a cork; something is intriguing him. I stop at a large rock and examine it in the dim light. I make out a faint inscription carved into it. I stand up and look around. It's a cemetery, with the upturned rocks used as headstones. Prince trots over to a mound of earth. It's freshly dug and he sniffs what's below. He must be smelling the newly dead. I'm relieved; the cemetrey means that we're close to a village and therefore the valley.

There's no time to stop. We have to cross the river before dawn but the difficult descent has put us several hours behind. I stroke Prince's head and he looks up at me from the grave, when there's a distant sound of shooting. I grab Prince and drag him with me to hide behind a large headstone. I release the safety catch on my M4 and prepare myself. It's hard to know exactly where the shots came from. There are several more. I listen more carefully as the hope builds up in me that it may be a battle between the Taliban and our troops. But it sounds more like small-arms fire than heavy combat weapons and rocket grenades. It stops and there's silence. Prince stares at me, as if wondering why we're hiding, because, of course, he hasn't heard the gunfire. I wait some minutes but there are no more shots. The little hope I had that the allies may be nearby is gone. In all probability it was a quarrel between local warlords over a matter of honour or money; I've witnessed such skirmishes before. At least the firefight happened far enough away for me to feel we will be safe.

As we take a well-worn path down the slope from the cemetery, the sun comes up, slowly at first and then in a bright dazzle of light that makes me squint. Prince is walking in front when I almost topple over him because he's suddenly stopped. I hit the stony ground hard and can feel immediately that I've hurt my chin. I sit up on my knees and feel for any break, only to hear footsteps not far away. I look up and see Prince staring ahead. A figure is coming up the slope towards us. I grab my rifle and get ready to shoot.

Instead of a man coming towards us it's a boy about five or six years old. He's got a black vest on and white linen trousers which, as he comes closer, I see are splashed with blood. The boy walks straight at us. The fear he may be a suicide bomber grips me. I point the rifle at him and tell him to stop but he doesn't. As he comes closer I yell out again, this time in Pashto, ordering him to stop. Still he continues coming. I glance at Prince, who is rigid, his lips quivering as if he's smelling whether the boy is friend or foe.

I yell out again but the boy keeps coming at the same steady pace, and as he does I notice how blank his face is. Prince growls softly. I tap him to be still.

By the time the boy is a few metres away I realise that he seems in a total daze. He walks past us as if he isn't aware we exist and heads towards the cemetery. He has no food, no water. He's certain to die in the heat. I run after him and grab him by the shoulder. He doesn't look at me, and shrugs me off. I grab him again and turn him to face me.

His eyes have the thousand-metre stare of soldiers who have been through a terrible battle. The blood on his trousers is drying a dark red and one of his leather sandals is covered in donkey dung. Maybe he saw or was part of the firefight. He doesn't seem aware of me wiping away the blood on his cheek and forehead with my sleeve. Suddenly he jumps away, yelping in fright when he sees Prince. He stands a few metres away, staring at me and Prince as if he cannot believe his eyes. *It's all right, it's all right, we're not going to hurt you,* I say in English. He spins around in a panic as if he's aware for the first time of where he is. I hold out my hand to him. He doesn't move but trembles as he stares at Prince. I wave Prince away and hold out my hand again. *Come on, let me take you home.*

I take his limp hand and start to walk him, but he pulls away. I drop down on one knee and touch his cheeks. *Come on, mate, I'm taking you home.* I stand up and as I do the boy's face goes blank as if in shock again. He doesn't seem aware of where he is and who I am any more. Prince looks at the boy, as if trying to understand what is going on. I motion him to lead and the boy and I, hand-in-hand, follow. His hand is so tiny that it makes mine feel huge, like a wicket-keeper's glove.

According to the map there's a village somewhere near the river we are going to be crossing. The boy may have come from there or maybe not, but I'll drop him off as close as possible to the village without Prince and me being seen.

He walks beside me, his eyes fixed somewhere on the horizon or beyond to a place only he can see. He says nothing when I speak to him and keeps a steady pace. I pause a couple of times to give him water. I have to squeeze open his mouth to pour water down his throat. He doesn't complain and doesn't flinch when I touch him. It's as if his body is here but his mind is elsewhere. Whatever he has seen, he has been badly traumatised by it.

Eventually we round a switchback and suddenly the valley is below, down a steep slope. There are crops but most of the fields are ploughed or left to pasture. In the distance is a small village surrounded by mud walls.

It's slow going moving in a zigzag fashion down the hill. One time I slip on some stones and trying to balance find myself sliding forward on my back. When I stop, I realise I'm still holding on to the boy. He stares listlessly at the sun. I lift him up and point to the village. *Home*, I say. *You'll soon be home, Sonny Jim.*

With Prince still leading we reach the outskirts of the village and hide in some long grass. The countryside is too open for me to get any closer without being seen. I motion Prince to stay and I walk the boy to the dirt road that leads to the compound. I let go of his hand. His eyes focus on the ground as if seeing beneath it to an underworld below. I lift up his head so he faces the village. *There*, I say, *there's your home*. I point and tell him to go there. I step away and he stands rooted to the spot as if he has no will of his own. I don't know how to wake him up to his situation. There's only one thing I can do. I spit in his face. At first he doesn't react but when I do it a third time, he jumps as if waking from a dream. He looks bewildered to see me and wipes the spittle away, and for a moment examines his hand as if he half expects to see blood. He looks back at me and a flicker of anger crosses his face. I point again to the village. He follows the direction I'm pointing in. *You go. You go home!* I order. He nods, as if understanding, and in that even pace of his, he starts towards the village.

I return to my hiding place to watch his progress, to make sure nothing dreadful happens to him. The plan is to cross the river and head across the plains opposite. I hear the distorted and distant cry of a mullah, over a tinny public-address system, calling the faithful to prayer. His voice is drowned out by the sound of a motorbike. I see a bike on the dirt road, with a driver and his pillion passenger, both dressed in Taliban black with white turbans, rifles slung over their shoulders, heading towards the boy a hundred metres away. The motorbike stops and both men get off and talk to him. I don't know what he is saying, if anything, until he turns and points in my direction.

It's strange but I am not surprised he's told them where I am. I don't blame him. I'd have done the same if I was his age. The driver and passenger jump back on their bike. It roars into life, veers off the road and races straight towards me, bumping over the rough soil of a ploughed paddock. The passenger aims his rifle. There's a shot, and a puff of dust rises near my feet. *Come on, Prince*, I shout. Prince sees me making a dash towards a crop of green maize and runs after me.

The maize is shoulder-high and I leap into it as a shot buzzes over my head. I hear Prince behind me squeezing his way between the dense rows of stalks. I push my way through the crop towards the middle. The driver has switched off the bike and everything is quiet. I crouch amongst the thick green stalks and leaves, so as not to be seen, and listen carefully. My skin is prickling with fear. Prince is gazing up at me for some sort of answer or reassurance. I make the hand gesture for him to be quiet and pat him.

There's the faint rustle of leaves to my right and a second later a similar sound coming from in front of me. The crunching sound of feet on stalks becomes louder. Where do I aim? Right or straight ahead? Prince starts growling. I'm about to stop him, because he's giving our position away, when he barks at something. I look to my left. A man in black is pushing his way through the maize. He stops a couple of metres away, as surprised to see us as we are to see him. He lifts up his rifle. I go to aim mine but my arm won't move. I look down and it's caught up in the thick clump of stalks. As I frantically try to pull my rifle free, Prince leaps at the soldier. There's a loud sharp crack and Prince twists backwards in mid-jump as a bullet hits him. He drops to the ground and is still.

The Taliban points his gun at me but by now I have freed my arm and I fire. The bullet hits him in the chest. He grunts loudly and slumps, but does not fall because his body is caught up in the stalks. He doesn't move. I push through the maize to Prince. He's lying on his side, blood pouring out of a hole in his neck. I can't believe it; he saved my life and now he is dying. Two shots ring out and bullets rip into the leaves near my face. I fire blindly in the direction of the shots. There's a cry of alarm and loud rustling sounds, as if the man is running away in panic. I don't have much time. I have to get Prince and myself out of the maize.

His eyes open and he staggers to his feet, only to flop down. I drop my rifle, lift him up, and wrap him around my shoulders as I have seen Casey do when practising to prepare for an emergency like this. He's heavy and I begin staggering. I'm dry-mouthed with shock, and telling myself to breathe. Breathe to help me be calm, breathe to help me carry my load, breathe to live, breathe to save Prince.

I make it to the edge of the crop, where I pause and carefully take a step out into the open and look around. I can't see the second man. He must be on the other side of the field, where his motorbike is. This gives me a little time to examine Prince. I place him gently on the earth and kneel beside him. His eyes are half closed and he's panting with pain. The blood from his neck is slowing to a trickle. I turn his head and I'm stunned to see that there is another bloody hole on the opposite side of his neck, only smaller, where the bullet has exited.

He'll die unless I can get him help. I grab the last of the Quick Clot from my medical kit to powder his wound then I hear footsteps running on the hard earth. The Taliban soldier is screaming something in his own language as he sprints towards us, pointing his gun at me as I'm kneeling next to Prince. I feel for my rifle, only to remember I left it in the maize. I fumble for my pistol, when I hear a shot.

The force of the bullet throws me onto my back. The pain in my left side is excruciating, as if I've been branded with white-hot metal and it's searing my flesh. Time seems to slow down. I feel the wound at my side and glance at my fingers; they're scarlet with blood. I'm suddenly overwhelmed by a desire to sleep, but my bloodied hand, as if acting independently of me, grabs my pistol from where it had fallen to the ground. Things are becoming dreamlike, as if everything around me is no longer real. The man who wants to kill me shouts something again and takes a couple of steps closer to have a clearer shot at me. I have no time and point my Glock in his general direction and press the trigger. There's a slight recoil. The Taliban soldier moans in agony, drops his rifle and clutches his right thigh near his groin. He grimaces and then, on seeing me taking aim again, hobbles away as quickly as he can. I fire two shots more but miss. He vanishes around the side of the crop.

I notice a movement and am amazed to see Prince trying to stand. He's shaking his head as if trying to rid himself of a painful migraine. I can feel the warm blood from my wound seeping down the inside of my left trouser leg. I unbutton my shirt and am horrified to see that a large piece of flesh, the size of a golf ball, is missing from my left side. Blood is pouring out of the gash. The pain is almost unbearable and I yawn to stop from fainting.

The motorbike roars into life and it appears from the other side of the maize, crossing the ploughed paddocks, the driver bouncing up and down as he heads towards the road. Once he reaches it he turns south towards the village. It won't be long before the alarm is raised and more Taliban will be coming after us. The driver is going fast, leaving an enormous dust trail behind him. We've got to get out of here.

I'm putting my revolver back in my belt when I hear an explosion. I look up and see the bike and the driver disappear in a puff of black smoke. It takes me a few moments to realise that the bike has hit a roadside mine. There is no way he would have survived such an explosion. The only thing I feel is a sense of relief that the death has given us a little more time.

12

There's a chance that the bullet that passed through Prince's neck hasn't damaged any vital organs. I can't look at him for fear of breaking down. He has saved my life but at a terrible cost.

Working quickly, I cut the legs off my trousers and wrap them around my torso, hoping this will stem the bleeding. The trousers become soggy with blood. Pain almost causes me to pass out. I search for a morphine tablet in my medical kit, but they're all gone. I have no time to retrieve my rifle. All I have is my pistol and knife.

Come on, boy, we have to go. His eyes are dull with agony as he walks slowly beside me. When we reach the stream I fill the water canteen and Prince drinks deeply. There's a hill ahead of us and beyond that nothing, just treeless plains. The day is heating up and it will be a gruelling march to reach our target, a village that should be somewhere to the east.

After crossing the stream, we walk up the slope. Our progress is slow. My blood loss is making me weak and Prince seems to be in pain every step. It would be so easy just to stop and give in, but I will myself on, as if commanding myself to do it, just as Prince seems determined not to stop either, because if we do, we will die.

The sun is so bright that it becomes a white light, blinding and painful. Sometimes I look behind to see if we are being followed. I'm in despair at how little distance we have travelled. Only our footsteps are signs of life in the dirt, as if we are the first and last living things on a dead planet. My body throbs with soreness as if every part of it has been pummelled. Prince's head is beginning to droop and his limp grows worse.

The desolate earth before us begins to shimmer, as if it has become the ocean. I know it's a mirage but it has a reality that is hard to shake. The sight of the sea drives me on. Once or twice I collapse to my knees with exhaustion and pain. Prince waits patiently for me to struggle to my feet and then we move on again through the furnace.

Soon we are not in a desert but seem to be on a beach walking down to the sea. I hear myself whispering, *Thalatta! Thalatta!* The sound of the jingle trucks swirl around in my head. I spin around, half expecting to see a convoy of them chasing us. But there is nothing. I cough up blood but do not care. *Right foot . . . left foot*, I tell myself, as I try to concentrate on the simple act of putting one foot in front of the other.

I stop for a moment to try and find any sign of a place where we can shelter from the heat and recuperate, but there's only the beckoning sea. I sorely need to rest. I'm about to move off again when I sense that Prince is not with me. I look back and see he has stopped some twenty metres behind. I hobble back to him. He's lying on his side, with the black film of his eyes peeled back revealing his true blue eyes, but they're not sparkling; their beauty is dulled with pain. His tongue is lolling out. He's close to death. I spit on his face trying to get a rise out of him, but he doesn't care any more and only sighs. I find myself shaking him and screaming out his name, but he doesn't move.

I kneel in the hot earth, staring at him, and begin to weep. I take out my revolver. I can't leave him behind in pain, to die alone. It will be better to kill him and then myself. I aim at his head, but my finger can't press the trigger. I hear a tinny sound, like mechanical mosquitoes and I see two black dots, with large dust clouds trailing behind them, heading towards us. The glare is harsh and I squint to see properly. I make out two motorbikes, both with pillion passengers. I hear myself groan with despair. We'll never escape the Taliban. They will keep at us until we're killed. There's no way out, Prince and I are going to die in this godforsaken land. I don't know what date it is, but I'm going to die before I reach nineteen.

The realisation that I will die strangely calms me. I pull out the pistol and fill it with bullets. What amazes me is how steady my hands are. How detached I feel. I aim at the motorbikes and start shooting. I don't feel any recoil. It's as if the revolver is an extension of my arm, they're both one and the same. A bullet hits the first driver and his motorbike spins out of control and accidentally rams the other one. The collision flings the riders and passengers onto the ground. Nobody moves for a moment and then three Taliban emerge from the dust cloud and run to the fourth who lies still.

There's probably enough time for me to put some distance between us. I slip my gun back in its holster and with a supreme effort and buckling knees, I lift Prince up and wrap him around my shoulders. I'm determined we will live or die together. He's so heavy that I stagger under his weight and almost drop him. I steady myself and begin to march. The warmth of his belly against the back of my neck consoles me; it means he is still alive.

We make our slow way towards the sea. The grey earth and blue sky meet at the horizon and I find myself on the sandy floor of the ocean. I'm Captain Nemo walking on the bottom of the sea. I have a strong sense we are being followed and, turning around, I spot three black sharks on our trail, only fifty or so metres behind us. They look scrawny and hungry, eager for us to drown. I can't shoot at them because that would mean I'd have to take Prince down from my shoulders, but I know, with a certainty, that if I do then I won't have the strength to lift him up again. All I can do is keep moving. Insects buzz and whistle around my ears as the Taliban shoot at us.

My right leg is covered with sea lice drinking the blood that's leaking from my wound. The pain has gone. I don't feel my body or Prince's weight any more. I hear more buzzing and whistling around me. We're making our way through the water so slowly it's as if I'm wearing a bulky deep-sea diver's suit and heavy lead boots. The sea begins to shake and a terrifying noise, as if announcing an approaching sea monster, fills my ears. I try to stop myself from giving in to exhaustion but there is nothing I can do. My legs begin to wobble, as if their bones have been removed and I tumble to the ocean floor, Prince landing next to me.

I twist my body and glimpse the black sharks closing in on us. I look up at the surface of the blue sea and am amazed to see a gigantic sea spider falling rapidly towards us. Its mouth is wide open and it's going to eat us. My hand wraps around the handle of my pistol but I don't have the strength to pull the trigger. I lie on my back, Prince at my side, and wait to be taken. I'm past caring about the sharks and the spider. I'm beyond pain and feel as if my spirit is leaving my body. I'm comforted by the thought that we will perish together. I reach out and rest my hand on Prince. He bends his head and licks it. The warm, moist tongue feels beautiful.

13

There seems to be no difference between dreaming and reality, life and death. The world is darkness and in it I hear scraping noises, echoing footsteps, the soft voice of a woman, a puffing sound and distant men whispering – are they whispering about me?

Light comes and I see I am in a bed and my arm and chest have tubes attached to machines. I'm confused and then slowly realise I am in a bed in the army hospital. Now I remember – Prince and I were saved.

I learned later that an American drone had spotted an allied soldier and a black dog. It was only after the Australians recognised us in an aerial photograph that they realised there were survivors from the raid. A helicopter was sent to rescue us. I don't remember the ride back to base, all I can recall is the anesthetist injecting my arm and Prince on a stainless-steel table next to me, with a tube running out of his mouth as a surgeon worked on him.

The nurse told me that my first words after waking from surgery were *Where is he?* She thought I was referring to Casey, but it was Prince. After two days I had recovered enough to ask where he was, fearing he might be dead. A nurse told me he was still ill and being kept under observation in the vet's surgery. I was desperate to see him but the doctors thought I was too weak to move. The painkillers were affecting my mind and I've been told that I began to rant, saying that I was being lied to and that he was really dead. It was only after I threatened to pull out my intravenous dripline that I was lifted into a wheelchair and taken to the vet's surgery.

My body shook with anxiety. What if I was being lied to and far from recovering he was actually dying? I was wheeled through the operating theatre to the back room. The medical orderly opened the door and I took a deep breath, afraid of what I might find. In the middle of the room was a large cage and inside it Prince was lying on his side on a brown blanket, with a tube running into his mouth. Patches of his fur around his neck and flank had been shaved where the wounds had been stitched up. The only sign of life was the slight rise and fall of his chest. I called his name but there was no response. I began to cry, cry like a baby.

Every day I'd visit him and sit in a chair, still attached

to my dripline, just watching the rise and fall of his chest, hoping that he was getting better. But he seemed in a state of limbo, neither improving nor becoming worse. I'd keep vigil for hours, praying for him to get well.

The remains of those killed on the mission, including Casey, were eventually recovered. On the day Casey's body was to be flown back to Australia for the funeral, I stayed alone for an hour in the aircraft hangar beside the coffin draped with an Australian flag. *Casey, I told him, I always looked up to you. You were the one I always wanted to be like. Without your Prince, I wouldn't have made it. I promise you, Casey, from the depths of my heart, I will always care for your Prince. He's mine now but your spirit is inside him.*

I visited Prince and told him about the goodbye. I knew he couldn't hear and even if he could he wouldn't have understood, but I had to share the news with him. Maybe it was a coincidence but he opened his eyes and looked straight at me, his stump of a tail wriggling for a moment on recognising me.

A week later we were allowed to exercise and the two of us did circuits of the base every morning and evening, slowly regaining our strength. On one outing we were photographed and interviewed by reporters. Ours was called 'a feel-good story'. I didn't think it was. I had lost my friend, and a dozen men on the raid had been killed.

One afternoon I took Prince to Casey's room, which hadn't changed a bit. Prince sniffed the bed and under it, as if searching for Casey. When he couldn't find him he looked up at me, frowning, as if hoping I could supply the answer to the mystery. He stood before the bed for a minute or so as if trying to fathom his master's disappearance. Then he walked over to the locker and scratched at the door. *What is it, Prince?* I asked.

When he turned and looked at me with wide, questioning eyes, I immediately realised that he could hear. He was no longer deaf. I felt such a joy that it was as if my insides were flooded with light.

He scratched again and I opened the door. The locker was empty except for an object on the top shelf. I grabbed it and showed Prince, who gave a sharp bark of joy. It was a square rubber ball.

14

Emerald Creek looks the same. Most of the shops have closed, but the main store and hotel are still open. I turn the car off the main street and we drive up a winding gravel road. Beyond us is the snow-capped mountain, steam rising from it into the cold air. I glance at Prince sitting next to me. His curious eyes take in this new countryside. The fur is growing back over his healed wounds. His hearing is better but he still has a slight limp. It's typical of Prince that he doesn't seem too troubled by it.

We drive up a muddy track to the house. It still looks exactly the same. My father built it himself out of sandstone slabs and planted fruit trees in the back yard. The house stands alone on a small hill, weather-worn and looking older than it really is. We stop and get out of the car. I shiver in the cold air. The sky is a bright, fresh blue. I recognise the signs; it won't be long before it begins to snow.

I push open the rusty gate and Prince rushes up the

white gravel path. Dad knows we are coming but I still feel nervous. How will he greet me? Has he forgiven me for joining the army? I knock, as if at a stranger's house. I hear his heavy, even footsteps coming down the hallway. There is a pause, almost as if he is taking a deep breath like me, and the door opens. He looks weary, as if he hasn't slept for days. He stares at me and then at Prince, almost as if he can't decide we are real. I know I have to be the first to speak. *Hello, Dad. This is Prince. We've come home.*

He steps aside and motions us in. The house is warm from an open fire. He follows us into the living room and I hear him laughing. It surprises me. I turn around, wondering what he finds so funny, only to realise he is weeping. Before I can recover he leaps at me, almost as if wanting to hit me, but his arms wrap around me in a hug so tight I can barely breathe. I hug him and weep. *You're alive! You're alive!* he keeps on saying.

Once we stop crying and step away from each other, I realise it is the first time we've touched one another in years. A little embarrassed by our intimacy, Dad looks down at Prince, who is frowning, not understanding what is happening. *So this is the famous Prince I saw in the papers.*

We join him in his study. Without a word, he places a glass of soda water on the floor before Prince, hands

172

me a whisky and then pours one for himself. We clink glasses. *Welcome home, the both of you*, he says. We drink in silence while Prince laps up his water. I don't mind my father not talking because I sense his emotions are so deep that no words can explain them, and I feel the same. With a contented sigh, Prince lies down at my feet.

When I take Prince out into the front garden my insides are pleasantly warm. I grab his favourite toy from the car. I hide it behind my back and pretend I don't have it, but he knows. He jumps up and down in the same spot, eager to play. The winter sunlight catches his eyes, and they're a beautiful sparkling blue. I feel something wet land on my nose and look up. Snow is starting to fall and is dusting the garden white. I hold out the square ball and Prince barks with eagerness. I throw it across the lawn in a high arc. He runs after it, watching its flight, and then when it bounces leaps at it, missing, as it shoots off sharply in an unexpected direction. But on the second leap he grabs it.

Watching him trot proudly back to me, the square ball in his mouth, I feel a rush of love. And I think he feels the same. We're now inseparable and I cannot imagine life without him. He begins to run in ever smaller circles around me, his whole being filled with joy. I laugh with happiness. For us the war is over.

ACKNOWLEDGEMENTS

This story is fiction, though I consulted many books and articles during the writing of it. The best sources were American and English accounts of the war, most of them written by exceptional journalists and soldiers. A character like Ghulam, for example, is based on a fleeting description by a British reporter. There have been few such revealing and unflinching books written by Australians and it was difficult, if not impossible, to gain information I wanted from the Australian army, so Mark's medical kit, for instance, is based on that used by American dog handlers.

My wife, Mandy Sayer, gave me wonderful advice.

And a special thank you to Sarah Brenan for her painstaking and astute editing. All the mistakes are mine.

LOUIS NOWRA is a playwright, novelist and screen-writer. He lives in Sydney with his wife, the writer Mandy Sayer, and their dogs, Coco, a Chihuahua, and Basil, a miniature Pinscher. They live in Kings Cross, a place he has written about extensively in his recent *Kings Cross: A biography*. His previous YA novel was *Into That Forest*.

Two young girls go into
that forest and come out
changed forever.